Feather's Girl

Jacquelyn Johnson

©2020 Crimson Hill Books/Crimson Hill Products Inc.

All rights reserved. No part of this book, including words and illustrations may be copied, lent, excerpted or quoted except in very brief passages by a reviewer.

Cataloguing in Publication Data

Jacquelyn Johnson

Feather's Girl

Description: Crimson Hill Books trade paperback edition | Nova Scotia, Canada

ISBN:	978-1-989595-58-9 (Paperback – Draft2Digital)
BISAC:	YAF000000 Young Adult Fiction: General YAF022000 Young Adult Fiction: Girls & Women YAF058020 Young Adult Fiction: Social Themes – Bullying
THEMA:	FXB – Narrative Theme: Coming of age YXO -- Children's / Teenage personal & social issues: Bullying, violence, abuse & peer pressure YXHB -- Children's / Teenage personal & social issues: Friends & friendship issues

Record available at https://www.bac-lac.gc.ca/eng/Pages/home.aspx

Front Cover Image: Cristina Zabolotnii

Book Design & Formatting: Jesse Johnson

Parts of this story formerly appeared in the novel Morley & Feather published in 2019.

Crimson Hill Books
(a division of)
Crimson Hill Products Inc.
Wolfville, Nova Scotia
Canada

Crimson Hill
Books

As Morley Star's 11 birthday dawns she's convinced her wish to adopt the rescue cat she's fallen in love with will finally come true.

Surely finally getting Feather as her own is the big surprise her mother has promised?

But Morley is about to have a very different birthday and summer vacation than the one she's hoped for. There will be surprises and secrets revealed as she learns what it really takes to make your fondest wishes come true.

A sweet middle grade story about being a modern girl who dreams big, friendship, family and finding out who you truly are, second in the Morley Stories Series for readers ages 10 to 13.

Also In
The Morley Stories
Series:

Just Me. Morley

Feather's Girl

Gifted

Rules for Flying

Find them all at
www.CrimsonHillBooks.com

"Hope" is the thing with feathers

That perches in the soul

And sings the tune without the words

And never stops - at all.

- Emily Dickinson

one

On the day before my 11th birthday, Sam sends an email saying she hopes I finally get Feather. He's the kitten I want to adopt from the pet shelter. I'm pretty sure that getting him is going to be my surprise gift.

I've wanted to adopt Feather for so long, to finally get him is so exciting I feel like I'm going to burst with happiness, just thinking about it.

In just one more day.

It will be...

The first time I get to cuddle him at home. Our home, not at the shelter where he's been for three months.

The first time he sits on my lap, purring, while I'm drawing or making bracelets. Or maybe he'll want to sit on my desk and watch.

The first time he curls up beside me while I'm falling

one

asleep.

I've pictured this in my mind and also in my sketch book so many times that to have it be true at last is...well, it's the best thing that's happened this year. Or maybe in my entire life!

Or it will be. In just one more day. Just one more. I'm counting the minutes!

Sam's letter says she's in Tuscany now, a place in Italy. It's where lots of movie stars have fancy homes. She's staying in one of them. It used to belong to a famous singer.

It's a palazzo. That's the name for a house that looks like a palace. She says she's having a great time. She sent my present and really hopes I like it.

Jayden, my other best friend, sends postcards with pictures of all the places they stop on their trip. He writes to say he's pretty tired of living with his parents in a little tin can trailer, but that it is interesting to drive across the country, especially when they were going through the Rocky Mountains. And he likes having so much time with his mom.

He says he mailed me a gift and to tell him all about my birthday. And how much he misses me and Sam and his horse, Spirit. But not school.

I've been away from home too, spending a week with my favourite aunt at her place. My Aunt Eira called it a time out for me and for my mother.

Things aren't much different at home. It's still hard to get along with my mother, and I don't think it's because she's going to have a new baby.

My little sister, Daisy, is still roaring around. My mother is still cranky a lot, mostly with me. We still have the BnB guests to look after, and all the baking she does and the jewellery I make to sell at the market on Saturdays. We still don't know when Danny's going to visit, exactly. He's Daisy's father, but not mine.

Mom did decide to go to the police about me being bullied by Julia Maclean, a girl in our grade but she's a year older than me and my friends.

My mother took the pictures that Eira took of my front and my back and my arms, showing the bruises I got from Julia hitting me. I had to tell the whole story again, to the police.

But then a strange thing happened. Some dog-walking people who where there when Julia attacked me also went to the police. The man said when he looked more closely at the video they made that day with their phones, it looked like two kids were fighting in the background. When they looked really closely, it looked like one of the kids was that girl who did the videos about why kids need pets and pets need kids, and also how to get your pet that are on YouTube.

He meant me.

Then the police looked more closely at that video.

And saw that everything I've been saying about Julia is true.

I wasn't the one who hit her and ripped her clothes and did the cut on her face, like she told everyone. She attacked me. Just like she has been doing since

one

she moved here for grade 4.

It was embarrassing that strangers saw me getting beat up. And crying.

And to find out that the police showed that video to Mr. Maclean. That's Julia's dad. Also our school principal, or he was last year, at Seabright Primary.

My mother is surprised about the video.

She doesn't apologize to me about not believing me about the bullying. Not exactly.

But she does stop being mad at me all the time. And to tell the truth, I don't really want to talk about the bullying. Or not to her.

So I ask her about the new baby. She says she's happy about it.

She says she feels like it might be a boy, this time.

She says she knows it means extra work from me and she'll even expect Daisy to help out.

She says it is so exciting and wonderful for us to be getting a new baby brother. Or sister.

I don't ask her about Danny coming home any more. He's been gone for months and never comes to visit, though sometimes Daisy goes to see him. I figure Danny's not coming back to be with us. Even though I'm pretty sure he is the new baby's father.

I do ask my mother about my father. I've never met him. I don't even know his name or where he lives or anything about him. Usually, she just tells me never mind about him. So it's a surprise when she tells me that she loved him very much, once. When they were young. Maybe too much. And she thought he loved her. Just not enough.

He lived in Ireland, not here. When she knew him.

She has no idea where he is now.

She tells me his name is Malcolm. That's his first name. And she says maybe when I'm a bit older she'll maybe try to find him. Maybe we could search for him together. Some day. When I'm older.

She says maybe she should have told me this sooner. But she didn't think I was old enough to understand.

She says she worries that I'm still not mature enough to understand. That's why she won't tell me his last name, she says. Because it could just stir up trouble.

But she knows where he lives. Or used to live.

Doesn't that mean he knows where we live?

But then why doesn't he come to visit? Is he a bad man, maybe even in jail so he can't come to Seabright to see me?

Or just someone who doesn't like kids? And doesn't even want to be a dad?

What if he's a good guy and he's tried to find us, but he can't?

Mom just shrugs when I ask. I think maybe she knows the answers, or some of them. But she doesn't like to talk about things, or at least not things I think are important. She'd rather talk about making cookies and what we need to do next for the guests that stay at

one

our house and what chores I have to do next. You know, ordinary stuff.

I don't ask her about Feather. I think getting him must be my big birthday surprise. I don't want to spoil it.

I wake up on the day of my birthday really, really excited. Today's the day, finally, when I KNOW I'll bring Feather home. I'm so sure that's what I'm getting, because the wish bracelet for getting him broke, didn't it? That's the magic about wish bracelets.

Even though it was Julia who broke it on purpose, I think my wish bracelet should still work. Because that's what wish bracelets are meant to do. They break and then the wish you made the very first time you put them on comes true.

I've made hundreds of them and sold them at the market. That's what I always tell people who buy them.

Everything is ready for Feather to come home. I have his litter box set up and food dishes and food and some toys.

I've got the pet carrier, to bring him home.

And I've read all about having a cat and what they need and how to care for them. Because of the Get A Pet Project, I know a LOT about cats. And because of being a volunteer at the pet shelter, I know a lot about being a responsible pet owner.

I hurry through breakfast and try to make Daisy hurry, too. I know the pet shelter opens at 10 a.m. We're ready long before that.

But then, my mom just starts baking. And says we can go get whatever it is I want for my birthday dinner.

There's no party. I already knew that. How could I have a party without my two best friends being there? Most of the kids I know are away for vacation. Aunt Eira and her boyfriend, Dom, have gone up north to his parents' cottage for two weeks.

My other aunt, Sorcha, and her kids have also gone away, to see their grandparents in Winnipeg. There's nobody to celebrate with except my mother and Daisy.

The three of us go out for lunch. I get to pick where. I choose the Peony Garden. It's got Chinese food. I really like the chicken fried rice and you get fortune cookies.

As I'm chewing my honey chicken, I wonder what Sam and Jayden are doing right now. Probably not eating lunch, because it's a different time where they are. I know, because I looked it up. Time for breakfast where Jayden is now, out in Vancouver. It's already night in Paris, where Sam is. I really wish they were here.

My fortune cookie says, "You will soon receive a gift of great riches." I haven't been thinking about being rich. I want a gift of great furriness.

Daisy's says, "Sweetness and joy will light up the days of your life." I guess that's already true for her. Mostly. She's already as happy as her name, when she's getting her own way.

one

Mom doesn't say what her fortune says. She just reads it, frowns and says, "They're just silly," and stuffs it in the pocket of her shorts.

After we eat, she pulls out a bag of gifts. I wonder if we're going to the shelter to get Feather right after lunch. Or if he'll already be at home when we get there, because she says the big gift from her and Daisy is at home, in our room.

My gift from Sam is a wire jewellery-making kit with lots more bracelet designs in it, plus a gift certificate to the craft store. Jayden sent me a book of funny facts about pets and a poster of kittens and cats.

Mom says I can choose what colour frame I want for my poster. Danny sends a card with money in it and so does my grandfather. Mom says that can go straight to my bank savings account.

Eira and Dom also got me a card. Inside, there's a certificate for 12 art lessons with Maudie Lewis, a local artist whose work really blows me away. I'm super excited to meet her and get to paint with her.

Daisy gives me a card with lots of fairies playing with dancing kittens. It gives me an idea for a bedtime story for her. But maybe, this time, I should write it down and draw it, like a graphic novel. Or, better yet, let her draw it.

Now that it's summer, one of my jobs is thinking up fun stuff for her to do so mom gets lots of baking time and some rest time. Daisy drawing a book of fairy pictures could keep them both happy for a while, I think.

When we leave the restaurant, we drive to the craft store, where I pick out some more jewellery-making supplies and a frame for the poster Jayden gave me. Then I think we must be going to the pet shelter. But instead, mom turns towards home.

"Look in your room to find your gift," she says when we get there. "I know you're going to love it!"

I run down the hall. "Feather?" I call. "Feather?" I look all over, but don't see him. And I don't hear him, either, in my head.

Is he hiding? I can't tell.

My mother comes into our room behind me. "Isn't it pretty? I really hope it fits," she says.

It fits? Then I see it, on my bed. It's a new bathing suit with green and purple splodges and huge pink and red flowers. And there's a matching stretchy beach skirt. And a pink sun hat. And a new pair of sunglasses. And a bright pink tee shirt, with a skinny white cat on it. The cat is wearing pink sunglasses.

 "I know how disappointed you were that you couldn't swim at your friend's party. But that's the last cast you're going to have on your arm, so soon you can swim again. I know you've missed it. I thought you'd love a new suit."

It's just about the ugliest bathing suit I've ever seen.

"So, are you going to try it on?" Mom says. "Isn't it so cute?"

No, it's not. It's hideous. Like the most ugly wallpaper you've ever seen. Times a thousand. But you're never

one

supposed to say that, about a gift.

I don't know what to say. It isn't anything like what I'd pick out, if I was going to get a bathing suit, which I'm not going to put on. Not until the bruises are gone. Plus, putting on a stretchy tight thing like a bathing suit is still really hard, with one good arm and one kind-of weak arm in a cast.

I might be able to get it on. But, after swimming, when your swimsuit is wet and plastered to your body, it's even harder to get off than it was to get on. I'm not going to let my mother or anyone else help do that.

"But…it's not Feather." I say. "You said wait-and-see about getting him and I did wait. And wait. For a really long time. So I thought…"

"Feather? What are you talking about?"

"Feather, the kitten…"

"At the shelter? No, Morley. I told you, we aren't getting any pets. So please just stop whining about it. Believe me, I have my reasons for no pets. Very good reasons…"

"What are they?" I say, shoving the ugly bathing suit aside so I can sit on my bed. I wish she'd just take it back to the store. "Because I explained for every single reason you had to say no, there was a way to not have that problem. It was all in my pet project presentation. Everything, even how I can pay for Feather, so I thought you ca…"

"I'm sorry, Morley," she says, interrupting me. "Listen to me. Now isn't the right time to get a cat. We've just had a lovely lunch out together and you have some beautiful gifts. Why don't you have a look at them? You need to remember to be grateful for what you've got. And you have some Thank You letters to write too, don't you?"

Thank you letters are another rule at our house. You have to write them the same day you get a gift. Just saying, "Hey, thanks," in an email isn't enough, Mom says.

That would be if I could send an email. There's a no computer rule in our house, and I'm not allowed to use her phone. Also, I can't have my own phone.

I'm so disappointed, I want to cry. Or maybe yell at someone. I'm too upset to make jewellery, or draw something, or read, or do anything.

"Yeah," I said. "Maybe. Later. I'm, uh, going for a walk…"

"Fine. Be back by 4, because we're going to the beach. I promised Daisy…"

I grab my bike that Dom fixed almost like it was after Julia stomped on it and head for the pet shelter.

There, I check on Feather. He's still in his cage, curled up, falling asleep.

Feather, I'm sorry. I'm so sorry, I tell him in my mind.

Girl. Gone, he says. Then he's sleeping.

I race through all the tasks they ask me to do, watching the clock. I get those jobs for the other pets done in record time, so I can have a long, long cuddle with Feather. I wash my hands and lift him out of his cage. I sink my face into his soft fur. His head smells like carnations and cinnamon.

Girl, he says.

Morley, I remind him. *I'm Morley*.

Want to go home, he says. *Take me home*.

He starts to purr. He has a really soft purr, so soft you have to be cuddling him to even hear it.

He looks up at me and puts one soft white paw on my cheek.

I whisper to him about what it will be like, when he comes home with me.

When he is mine.

And I am his.

I promise him that it will be soon. I say it out loud. Because I need to hear it. I need to believe.

Most of all, I need to hope.

two

At first, I was worried about Saturday Market days.

I don't mean about going there. I mean being there all morning to sell our cookies, jewellery and pet portraits.

Usually, I'm the kind of girl who likes quiet and doesn't really mind being by myself, just reading or drawing or doing crafts. Or being with just a few friends. But I'm not crazy about crowds.

The market is big and full of echoes on market day. It's like a barn but made out of red bricks, with a tin roof. It's always noisy and always cold in there, like a basement. Even in summer.

I worried that it would be hard to just sit in one place all morning and talk to strangers about cookies. Or bracelets. Or me doing a drawing of their favorite pet.

Most of the people at the market are adults doing

two

their shopping. Or they're the vendors. Some of the booths have teenagers selling, but I was the youngest vendor there.

I worried about it.

What if nobody wants to buy anything?

What if they think everything is too expensive?

What if I don't say the right things?

What if I give them back too much money, if they buy something? Or not enough?

Or what if they're rude and I forget to do what my mother is always telling me to do, just act better than they do?

I have to remember to not tell them what I really think, if they're rude, because usually that's something you should keep to yourself. I know that. It's just I can't always do it.

Pretty much all these worries about selling things at the market come true the first few Saturdays we're there.

The market is crowded. And noisy. And so cold we need to wear hoodies.

I do get tired of being smiley and nice to people, even when they aren't.

Some of them say things that are really stupid, like "I'll buy these cookies if you pick all the raisons out of them first."

Or, "Will that bracelet leave black marks on my arm?"

Or, "What time do you put everything you've got on sale for half price?"

Or, the one that I gave first prize for stupid, but mum just laughed, was the lady who said, "I'd buy these cookies but I'm allergic to sugar. Do you have them without any sugar in them?"

My bum got really sore from sitting so long on those beach chairs mom bought for our booth. That's what she calls it, even thought it's only two old kitchen tables pushed together and covered with table cloths. Then all the cookies, cakes, cupcakes, squares and tarts, plus my jewellery are spread out on the tables.

I probably did say some dumb things. And, a few times I think I gave someone too much money back.

I thought mom would be angry and I'd hear about it, but she just shrugged and said, "this is new for both of us, Morley. We're learning how to do it. We'll probably both make some mistakes."

That made me feel better.

Just about every Saturday morning, Aunt Eira stops by and helps us for a few hours. One Saturday, Mom wasn't feeling well. I guess she had a cold again. She called Aunt Eira to come help me at our booth and Mom went home to rest.

That day, we had cookies, cakes and pies to sell and also Nanaimo bars and date squares. Not much of the baking had sold yet, even though the first two hours are usually busy with the early bird shoppers. But that all changed when my aunt got there.

Aunt Eira is pretty and smiley, like Daisy. Or Mum,

two

when she's in a good mood.

As soon as mom left, my aunt rearranged our table display. Then, instead of sitting behind our table like we always do, she got out in front and talked to people and offered them free samples of the cookies and bars.

She talked to everybody. And smiled and laughed with them.

Some people didn't really want cookies, but they stopped to look at my bracelets. There were the wish bracelets with beads in every colour, but also the fancier friendship bracelets, the fairy bracelets and some that were silver or gold metal with sea glass.

The fanciest ones, made with real jade or turquoise or amber, also have silver charms. That day, I only had a few of these for sale, because they cost more to make and I wasn't sure if they'd sell.

But if they didn't sell, I have to admit that I liked them so much I'd be happy to keep them. Or maybe give them as gifts. I know Eira had her eye on one of them.

I was just handing a lady her cookies and change when a man came over and said "Hey, that looks like our cat Burglar. Get it? Cat burglar? Ha, ha, ha. Yeah, well, it's pretty good. I'll give ya five bucks for it."

I'm so surprised I don't know what to say. Couldn't he see that my picture of Feather had a sign asking for donations to Sunflower Pet Shelter?

Luckily, Eira is there. She steps closer to the man. "Morley can do a portrait of your pet and have it ready for you to pick up next Saturday..." she says.

"Naw...I don't need that. I just kind of like the look of that one," he says, jabbing his finger on the picture of Feather.

"This picture is already spoken for, I'm afraid. But this is Morley Star, the artist. She'll be happy to do a custom portrait of your pet, uh, Burglar, or a cat like this for her standard fee of $45."

"What?" the man sputters. "You've got to be joking. Some little drawing by a kid?"

"Morley is a professional artist, craftswoman and business woman," Eira says. She's still smiling, but now her voice is as steely as Mrs. Green's. Mrs. Green was our grade 5 teacher last year.

"That would be for a drawing, of course," Aunt Eira says. "If you want watercolours or oil, the fee is $95. And we can also frame it for you, ready to hang up, for an additional..."

The man says a word kids use all the time on the school bus or you might hear on late-night TV, but isn't allowed in our house. Red-faced, he walks away.

"Remember this, Morley," my aunt says. "Demand respect for yourself and for your work. Always. Because if you don't, people will think they can act badly, like that man just did."

And besides, I think, what a jerk! I really wouldn't want a picture I made in his house!

She pulls out another piece of white cardboard, the kind we use to write down the prices of the baked

two

goods, and in a pretty script she writes:

Special Today Only

Custom pet portraits

By local artist Morley Star

$35 black line drawing

$85 in watercolour

First 5 people who book!

By closing time, we've sold all the baked goods.

There are only three bracelets left, even though Aunt Eira insisted I wasn't charging nearly enough for my work and she increased all the prices.

And I have assignments for the five black line drawings and three of the watercolour portraits. Everyone who wants pet portraits paid half of the money right away. That's called a deposit, Aunt Eira explained. Paying a deposit proves they're serious about getting my work.

Later, after we pack up, go back to my house, unpack everything and put it away, we check on my mother, who's sleeping.

Daisy is at her friend Moira's house for a birthday party.

"Why don't we do something special, to celebrate?" Eira says. "Just you and me!"

"To celebrate what?"

"You and your mom becoming successful businesswomen with the baking and your jewellery and pet portraits. That's three things. And how good you're getting at making these beautiful bracelets and pleasing your customers, that's two more things.

"And, um, just that it's a beautiful sunny day out and we can have a late lunch together because we worked hard this morning. We've earned it!"

We go to Chrystina's, because they make the best chicken nachos and, on hot days like this, their patio deck is open. My aunt orders chowder, because she says she loves it but never bothers making it for herself. "But that might change..." she says, smiling like she knows a secret.

"So, tell me, how much money did you make today?"

"There's $75 in the donations tin for Sunflower Pet Shelter," I say.

"And how much for baking and bracelets and pet portrait deposits?"

I don't know.

"Well, you need to count all the money in the cash box. Figure out how much goes to your mother for the baked good and how much is yours for bracelets and art..."

I have a mouth full of nachos, so I just nod. Mom and I usually do this, after we get back from the market on Saturdays.

"Then you look at the money that's yours. That's

two

called your total takings, or gross revenue."

"I though gross meant like – ewww, ick that's really disgusting or like really ugly."

"When it's money, it means all the money you get for selling your products. So say you sell eight bracelets, and the price for each one is $8. What is your gross?"

I try to remember the eight times table in my head. Eight times eight. "$64," I say.

"Right. That's your gross. Not your net, which is your profit."

"Net? Like catching fish?"

It's not a very good joke, but she laughs anyways. "All the money you catch is you net profit. That's how much you make after you pay all your expenses. Expenses are all the things you need in order to make your product and sell it."

Oh. I never thought of that before.

"You mean expenses are things like buying beads and cord and drawing paper and paint?"

"Very good, you're right," my aunt says, reaching over to steal one of my nachos. "Let's say you sell one of your bracelets for $8. OK, so you've got $8, but not really."

"You don't?"

"Well, no. You have to pay for your art and craft supplies and also other things."

"What things?"

"Do you pay your mom for using part of her booth?"

"No…not really."

"You should. She rents the booth every week. You use part of it, so you should pay part of the booth rent."

"I guess that sounds fair," I say, wondering why my mother never mentioned it. Maybe because I help her make and wrap the cookies and I help her sell them. "I sold 23 bracelets today, and there's the pet portrait deposit money, and the donations for the pet shelter. But they're separate. I wrote everything down."

"Good," my aunt says. The food server comes over to our table with the bill and my aunt taps the server's phone with her credit card to pay. She says lunch is her treat but I can do the tip. I get a $5 bill out of my wallet and leave it on the table.

"You know how much money you made today, gross. That's all the money for jewellery sales and pet portrait deposits. You know how much it costs to buy your supplies. But what don't you know yet?"

How could I know what I don't know?

"Ok, I see you don't understand. Your mother didn't, either, until I showed her." I'd forgotten that my aunt went to university to study business. But why didn't my mother mention any of this about how to know about your money after Eira showed her?

There isn't time to think about that, because Aunt Eira is saying more things I want to hear.

"What we need is my computer. Let's go back to my place until it's time to go pick up your sister at her

two

friend's house."

My aunt shows me what she calls "running your numbers." She says every businesswoman needs to know how to do this or she can't be successful.

Basically, she says, it's keeping track of money you have to spend to buy supplies or pay helpers, if you have any. The money that comes in, the gross revenue, is all the money you get for selling your products or services. Services are doing things for people for money, like shoveling their driveways or dog-walking or babysitting or helping weed their gardens.

What I do is sell products. My products are bracelets and other jewellery. And art.

Using her laptop, my aunt sets up something she calls a spread-sheet. It's like a huge chart that has little spaces in lines and columns where you put in numbers like how much it costs to make the bracelets, now much they sell for and what each of the expenses is. When you do all this, you can see how much profit there is left after you pay for everything else.

There are rows for everything, like buying beads and charms and jewellery-making tools and how much time it takes to make them. My aunt says that time is a cost for a business. A cost is the same thing as an expense. I should be paying myself to do the work of making and selling the bracelets, she says, because there wouldn't be any products to sell if I didn't spend time making them.

The jewellery-making time is what Aunt Eira calls the labour cost for the business. She says I should figure out how much I'm going to pay myself, per hour, for doing the jewellery-making work. And not forget to put in the time it takes to buy supplies and sell at the market. Those are also labour time expenses.

"You take your gross sales or revenue, that means all the money people pay you. Minus the expenses, that's all the money it costs to make your bracelets. What's left down here," she points to the bottom of the spreadsheet page, "is your profit."

We look at the profit together. I'm pretty impressed. It looks like a lot of money to me.

"Not enough," my aunt declares. "It looks to me like you're still not charging enough for some of your bracelets, the fancier ones."

It seems like being a businesswoman can get complicated. It's harder than just having fun making crafts.

I hadn't thought of it like a business. More like just something fun to do, like a hobby. But it's not just a hobby now, Aunt Eira says. Not when people are depending on me to make them things for themselves, or maybe for gifts, and paying me money to get those things.

"Of course, it's hard sometimes to be in business," my aunt says. "But also exciting, most of the time. And just about never boring!"

I think of my mother, who's told me that her job as the school secretary is tiring and boring, just about all the time. But it's what she has to do, she says, to earn money. And I know that baking and selling at the market also makes her tired. But she never looks like she's bored when she's doing the baking business.

"What about scary?" My aunt never seems to be scared of anything.

"Yes, being in business can be scary. That's part of why it's exciting. Things can go wrong and, when you're in business, you're the one who has to fix the mistakes. And solve the problems, when they happen.

"Nobody really teaches you how to be successful in business. You just learn some basic skills, like you're doing right now learning how to sell things or make a spreadsheet or run your numbers. It's the only way you can know about how much money you're making.

"Those are the basics. Anyone can learn the basics, if they try. But not everyone is successful in business, because most of what you learn about being a businesswoman you just learn by doing it. And making mistakes. And being brave. And smart. Like you and your mum already are. And working hard, but I think you've got that covered!"

She smiles and hugs me. "OK, enough lessons for today. Let's go get your sister!"

That evening, I'm in my room, filling in the numbers on the spreadsheet Aunt Eira printed out from her computer. Under Expenses, I put in how much I've spent on beads and wire and other pieces to make my jewellery. I decide to offer my mother $15 a week for my part of our booth rent, and I put that in, also under Expenses.

I decide to pay myself $5 per hour for making

bracelets and figure out how many minutes it takes to make one bracelet of each type that I do. That helps me know how much it costs to make each one.

I add up how much money my business earned today.

With the bracelets profits and pet portrait deposits, I have a gross of $270. It's the most I've ever made at the Saturday market. AND there's another $75 to add to the donations savings that will go to the Sunflower pet shelter.

I'm pleased with this.

But I'm not quite sure about what my net profit is. Have I done it right? Did I forget to put in anything? I need more help from Aunt Eira.

It makes me happy to see that when I add my money to my new bank account there'll easily be enough for our family to adopt Feather. And buy all his food and everything he needs for the next few months.

I know this, because I've worked it out for the Get My Pet project. I remember that was one of my mother's important reasons for her No Pets Rule. How much pets cost. But she can't say that about our family getting a cat if having Feather is paid for entirely by ME, so she doesn't have to worry about it!

I start thinking that what Aunt Eira said about money makes sense for my pet project, too. I pull out a notepad and start writing down numbers for my Get My Pet expenses spreadsheet. I'm pretty sure my aunt will help me with it.

It's surprising to see how much it costs to have one little cat. But now I know exactly how many bracelets

two

I need to make and sell every month to pay for everything Feather needs to stay healthy and be happy.

three

Another day, I'm over at Aunt Eira's with Daisy. She's playing with their new kitten, Pixel.

Pixel looks a bit like Feather, but she's totally silver-gray, except for a white bib and a striped tail.

Feather is black and white. He looks like he's wearing a little tuxedo.

Aunt Eira shows me some things on her laptop while Daisy is showing Pixel her Barbies. All the Barbies have on fairy outfits Mom made for them.

Aunt Eira and I look at the videos that she and Dom made out of my Get A Pet talk and put on YouTube. They've got a lot more views and likes now. Then we look at the Sunflower Pet Shelter website. Dom is designing a new one for them, she says. She wants to know what I think should be on the website.

She asks me like I'm a grown-up and I have thoughts

three

and ideas that are worth listening to. That's the special thing about Aunt Eira, one of them. She treats me like a person. Not just a kid.

Then we talk about my bracelet business. I still sell some of the wish bracelets but people mostly want the fancier bracelets. Some people have asked me to make earrings or necklaces to match the bracelets. There are also more people asking for pet portraits.

We look at my business numbers. That's how much I'm selling, how many hours I spend on my jewellery business and how much money I'm making. We also look at my bank accounts. Now, there's one for my money and one for the donations to Sunflower Pet Shelter.

Eira has shown me how you can see how much money you have in the bank by looking online. It's amazing how many things you can do with a computer, making me wish even more that our family could have one. Plus, I think it's really interesting.

Then we look at Eira's blog. It's called DIVA Delish! It's all about being young and stylish and having fun but not spending a lot of money. "Kind of like me," Eira says, laughing.

There's beauty tips and things about clothes and doing your hair and how to put on a party. There are also posts on how to start a business. Or make gifts that are really special, but don't cost very much. Or how to adopt a rescue pet. Or have a fun on a date for less than $25. Stuff like that for teenagers and young adults.

We talk about what kind of bracelets I'm going to

make next for her to sell on DIVA Delish! We brainstorm some ideas together, which is really fun.

She wants to know if I can do exclusive designs. That means, just for her to sell. "They need to have your name on them," she says. "Maybe something like Jewellery By Morley. Or how about Morley Star Originals?"

"Sure," I say. "That's great!"

"Oh, and we need to think up a way to present them."

"What's that?"

"Well, put each piece in a little bag. Or a gift box. We could buy them. Or you could make them."

"And that's another Expense, isn't it?"

"It is," she says, "But why don't you think about it? And, how about we get some ice cream and see if your mum wants to meet us at the beach?"

"Yay. Ice cream!" Daisy shouts, leaping up and scattering her doll things all over, making Pixel run away and hide under the couch. "I want chocolate!"

four

Danny arrives a few days after my birthday. We didn't know he was coming. Or maybe Mum did, but she wanted it to be a surprise.

And it is, for me, because he's a different Danny than I remember, back when he lived with our family. He left just after Daisy's birthday. That was last winter.

He looks different. Taller, somehow. And he acts different.

He used to dye his hair blonde and dress flashy, in shirts with string ties and plaid suit coats, like those used car salesmen in TV ads. But now, he just has on jeans and a tee shirt to some rock concert that happened long ago. He looks like a normal dad.

There's some gray in his brown hair, which I guess was always the real colour. He's wearing glasses, something he never did before. And he seems more serious, not always jokey and acting silly, like he used to.

He says he needs to talk to me and Mom, but first he needs to say some things to Daisy. Just her. So he figures she probably wants an ice cream sundae, doesn't she?

Daisy squeals and races to get into his car.

Mom looks disappointed.

I head upstairs to help her turn over the guest rooms. That means clean up after the last guests and make the rooms all super clean and neat for the next guests. We do this every day now. All four guest rooms have tourists in them every night. Mom has hired Aimee, a high school student, to help out for the summer.

Which is a relief because it means there's less work to do for the guests. For Mom as well as for me. We still have to do all the baking.

Every week we sell everything we make at the Saturday Market. AND take orders for more. It's crazy busy, but it's tourist season when there's always a lot of summer people in Seabright. They're the reason we're making a lot of money.

I know this because my mother bakes even more than she used to, and everything sells every week. I fill in all the numbers on the spreadsheets Aunt Eira made for me every week.

On Mondays, Mom and I take the market money to the bank. There's no more keeping money at home, in tins or her old purses like we used to do, she says.

four

That's just not safe.

I now have way more than I need for Feather saved up AND I'm giving money, from donations at the market and also from selling bracelets and the pet portraits, to the pet shelter every month.

When Danny and Daisy get back, Mum says I can entertain my sister for a couple of hours, so she and Danny can get a chance to catch up on a few things.

She says they have some serious things to discuss. Adult talk, she means. About us probably, but we're just kids so we can't know what they're saying.

I get Daisy working on fairy story pictures and sit down to do some more of the new-design bracelets, the ones Aunt Eira is going to sell on her blog. I try out making some of the little tags that will go on each one. I've decided that what they'll say is, "A gift for you by Morley Star."

Mom and Danny still aren't back by dinner time, so I heat up soup in the microwave and make grilled cheese sandwiches. We eat while watching *Wreck-It Ralph*. Daisy likes to sing every song. Really loud. She knows all the words.

It's the next day when Danny comes over and says why don't we go for a drive? I think he must mean him and Mom, but he means me. "Yeah, sure," I say, wondering what Danny has to tell me. I'm pretty sure he's going to say stuff like *You're the oldest and you need to look after your sister and your mom, because she's pregnant, you know.* As if I could ever get away from knowing.

But that's not what he has in mind.

He starts off by saying he's sorry he missed my birthday. That's a surprise, since he never much noticed me, or my birthdays, before when he lived with us.

I thank him for the card and the money. And tell him Mum says I have to put it all in the bank. He looks surprised but doesn't say anything.

I ask if he's coming back to be with us.

No, he says. This is just a visit.

"Are you and Mum getting a divorce?" Like Sam's parents did.

"Something like that. A separation. It means living in two places."

I look at my fingernails, wishing I didn't bite them. Or maybe they'd look better with nail polish. "But maybe you'll stop the separation and be together again, sometime in the fut…"

"No, Morley. That isn't ever going to happen. But I always will be Daisy's dad and a friend to you and your mother. A good friend, I hope."

I think about this. I wonder what kind of friend he could be, if he doesn't live in Seabright. Or near here. Or hardly ever visits.

"Will you live near us?"

"No. 'Fraid not. I already bought a new place. In the city. With a friend of mine. We both own it. Together."

Oh. I wonder who this friend is. "Is that your new

four

girlfriend?"

"Um, no. A good friend. I'll visit. Often as I can."

"Did you find your new job there, in the city?"

"Sort of. Yes."

"Did you steal cars, when you lived here?"

That's what kids at school said. That Danny had to leave town because he got arrested and put in jail.

I thought this might make him really angry, but he just laughs. "No, Morley, I promise you I never stole any cars, or anything else. But it was important for a while for some people to think I stole those cars..."

"I don't get it."

"I'll tell you the truth, because I know you're a truthful girl and you deserve an honest answer. I was working to find the real thieves..."

"Like a spy?"

"More like an investigator. We knew there was a major car-theft ring operating in the Northeast. We didn't understand everything about how it worked, so..."

"So you pretended to be a car salesman to find out?"

"That's it exactly. I got a job selling cars."

"Are you a policeman, like on those crime shows on TV? You know, the ones about Mr. Big?"

He laughs. "I had no idea you're so well-informed, Ms. Star," he teases. "But yes, I'm an investigator."

"A police officer?"

"Yes."

"And it's a secret, isn't it?"

He nodded. "Absolutely. Yes."

"Even from my mother?"

"She knows some of it. But it is a secret from your friends and family and everyone else. I'm trusting you, Morley, to keep it a secret."

I notice then that without his contacts his eyes are gray, not blue. It makes me think about what else we don't really know about him.

"Some kids said you had to leave town because you were a dirty rotten thief." That was Julia and her followers, Candy and Tiffany, but I didn't need to tell him that.

"Probably just what they heard their parents saying. Not true, but we had to make it look like it was. For a while. Not any more. I'm sorry about kids saying mean things like that to you. But we had to do it that way."

"Why?"

"It made the real thieves get bolder. When that happens, bad guys get careless. They make stupid mistakes. And that makes it easier for us to catch them."

"And you did?"

"Well, me and our team did, yes. It took a lot of people to bring them down, a lot of time and a lot of

four

work, but we have the proof about what they did. They're going to jail, or they're already there. For a long time."

"Did you tell Daisy this?"

"Nope. Only you. And, like I said, your mom knows some of it. But I will tell Daisy, when she's older. I think she really is too young to understand, don't you?"

"She'd probably blab about it."

"Little kids do. Older kids, some of them, like you, know better. But let's talk about something else. How are you doing? You seem to be getting better from everything that's happened?"

So we talk about that. About Daisy jumping out of the treehouse and I tried to catch her and got hurt. But it was really just an accident. She didn't know what would happen when she tried to jump down from the treehouse.

About mean girl Julia and how she has to do counselling and community service for bullying people and beating me up. And maybe go to a different school. But that, right now, she still lives here in Seabright.

About middle school. And where Sam and Jayden are this summer.

About selling at the market.

And about Feather.

By then, we'd finished eating our sundaes. Danny says we can go see Feather on our way home, if I want.

I wish Danny had said he'd adopt Feather and give him to me. But now, he says, "Sorry, kiddo. It's up to your Mom."

So we have to say good-bye and leave Feather behind. In his cage. It's getting harder and harder to leave him at the shelter.

Later, lying in bed, I was thinking about what Danny said. I know he's Daisy's Dad. And he's the new baby's Dad, too.

And my friend.

Maybe.

But I think he was also a kind of actor, pretending to be a car salesperson. Was he also pretending to be in our family?

Was he pretending to be my mother's husband? Or her boyfriend? I don't remember them getting married, but I was only 4 when they got together, so maybe they did.

Was Danny just pretending to like us, all those years he was with us? Just so he could live in Seabright and do his police job to catch thieves?

Before he left, he gave me an email address and his phone number. If I ever need him, he said to call or write. Any time.

He said he was sorry he was gone so much, before.

He said I could count on him to help us.

I'm just not sure what that really means.

four

......

The next day there's story hour at the library. Mom says I can take Daisy and look at books while my sister is enjoying the story hour. The library isn't very far from our house, so we walk there.

All the way, I have an eye out for Julia, but there's no sign of her. I wonder if her dad took her away for a vacation. Like pretty much everyone else I know. It's strange that all kinds of tourists come here in the summer, but people who live here go somewhere else. Except us.

When we get back, I can hear Mom and Aunt Eira in the kitchen. I want to rush in and hug Aunt Eira, because I haven't seen her for two whole weeks.

Mom is saying, "I've got one child who is sweet and easy to love, and one that gives me nothing but worries and trouble."

I stop for a minute, knowing I shouldn't be listening, but I don't want Daisy to have to hear what Mom says next. Because I know she's going to talk about all the mess Daisy makes, and the noise she makes and how she always dawdles and makes everyone late for work or school and she's always breaking stuff like my arm when she jumped out of the apple tree and I tried to catch her, and…

But no. I'm wrong.

Really wrong.

"How many times have we had the police at the

house? And the scare she gave me, with bruised ribs and a broken wrist! And then losing the renters, all because of some CAT! And now all this carry-on about pets…and all this trouble about Julia Maclean! I don't even know if I'll have a job, after this!"

Aunt Eira doesn't say anything. She's a good listener.

"My God, Eira, that's my boss' daughter. My BOSS! Have you forgotten that? And how do you think I'm supposed to work with him after this? I just don't know how I'll go back to school? That is, if I even still have a job…"

I'm so shocked, I stand as still as a statue, like my feet are frozen and stuck to the floor. Because the "nothing but trouble" child my mother is talking about is ME!

Even though I'm always vacuuming the rugs and changing the beds and helping with the baking and making things fun for Daisy and weeding the garden and all the other things I do to try to help my mother and make her happy.

Because I know she's worried about us.

But now Eira is saying, "Eefa! Listen to me! You've got TWO delightful daughters who are both healthy, beautiful, smart and a credit to you as their parent. And they both love you and need you."

There's a pause. I imagine my aunt taking a sip of iced tea, or maybe it's coffee. Then she says, "Sometimes, I just don't think you realize how lucky you are! How many people would be so proud to have children like Morley and Daisy!

four

"As you say, one of your daughters has a sunny, easy-going nature. The other is more thoughtful and serious but also a kind, compassionate and generous person. And a gifted artist. They're both lovely…"

"Easy for you to say," my mom says, interrupting her sister. "You're not a mother, so how could you possibly know?"

"That's so unfair that I'll just ignore it because I know you don't want to be hurtful and mean-spirited," Aunt Eira says in her serious voice. "It's just that baby brain means your head is all over the place. But let me remind you, Eefa, you have TWO children who are very special. They BOTH rely on you.

"One sweet, sunny and spirited little girl. One curious, very smart and talented older girl who is so much more than you give her credit for. Wake up, Eefa, before you throw her away…like you did with…"

I don't hear what she says next.

"Don't!" My mother says. "Don't you dare say that…"

Aunt Eira is trying to hug my mother, who's pushing her away when I finally get my feet to take me into the kitchen.

I pretend like Daisy and I didn't hear a thing. Like we just got there.

And yes, I know listening at doors is wrong, because you might not like what you hear.

I don't think Daisy noticed anything. She was behind me and trying to untangle her necklaces from her hair and the front of her fairy dress.

I try to smile like I didn't hear anything. I say, "Hey, you're back, at last!" to Aunt Eira and hug her. I notice my mother isn't looking at me. Then I grab juice boxes and cookies for me and Daisy and say "Come on, Daze, I'll make you a *special* fairy bracelet that is only for the queen of the fairies if you tell me what colours you want."

"My name is Fae," she says. "Not Daisy." That's her latest thing, that we have to use her fairy name, not her girl name.

"OK, Fae," I say. "Come on. Mom and Aunt Eira are doing grown-up talk. We're outa here!"

Aunt Eira laughs. Mom just turns away and shoves a tissue into her jeans pocket.

But the whole time I'm thinking, my sister is easy to love.

I'm nothing but trouble.

That's what my mother said. So, it must be true.

It makes me feel small.

And sad.

It's even worse than being invisible.

five

With making bracelets and baking and looking after the guests upstairs and selling things at the market and volunteering at the pet shelter and going to the beach and gathering sea glass and going for hikes and hanging out at Aunt Eira's, there never seems to be any time to just laze around and daydream.

I thought I'd have some vacation days to do nothing, but it never happens.

And then it's August and one of the hottest days of the year. I'm thirsty and sweaty when I get to the pet shelter. But there's a sign on the door saying:

CLOSED

until further notice

due to panleukopenia.

See website for details.

Closed? But how could the shelter be closed? Didn't the animals need to be cared for? And get adopted?

I knock on the door.

And wait.

And knock again.

Finally, someone comes. It's Heather, one of the vet techs. But she wouldn't let me in.

"I'm sorry Morley. Didn't you get the email about the pan-LUKE?"

No, I didn't get the email. How could I? We don't have a computer at home. It must have gone to Aunt Eira. Or Mum's phone. And why would a pan have anything to do with closing the shelter? "Pan luke? What's that?"

"Wait a minute. I'll come out." She does that, locking the door behind her.

Pan luke, she says. Short for panleukopenia. It's a virus that cats get. Like flu, but worse. Humans and dogs can't get it, but when cats do, it's very dangerous. Especially for kittens, because they haven't gotten their shots yet, the one that helps protect cats from getting this terrible illness.

There isn't any cure.

"But Feather...um...Shane," I say. "He's OK, isn't he? Please, tell me he's all right..."

five

"Shane? Little tuxedo cat? Yes, he's OK. He's one of the cats in Room A, and we're watching them..."

"What do you mean, watching?"

"It's a very, very contagious disease, Morley. It spreads quickly, but it takes several days to know which cats have it and are getting sicker. And some get it, but they survive. That's why we've had to close the shelter, until we can get rid of it."

"But all the cats will be OK?"

"No, I'm sorry, I can't promise you that."

"You mean, they could be really sick?"

"Yes. Some could die. But we're doing everything we possibly can to save as many as we can. I have to get back in there but...I'm so sorry Morley."

"But what can I do?"

"We just do everything we can and hope for the best, dear," she says as she slips back inside. "About all you can do now is pray for us!" Then she locks the door, with her inside with all the dogs and cats. And me on the outside.

Pray for them. Our family used to go to church all the time, but now we hardly ever go. I don't know if I remember how to pray.

I leave my bike in the rack and go around the back, to the window that I know is the one for Room A. Then I sit there, right under the window, and tell Lucky Feather to be strong. Because I'm counting on him to stay healthy so he can come home with me. And be my pet and my friend.

My best animal friend.

He must be frightened.

I know he's worried all the time, in that cage he's in, with all the strange smells and now, the smell of bleach. It's so strong, I can smell it coming out the window.

The smell must make it hard for the cats and dogs to eat.

But to get better, they have to eat. And drink water. And rest. Because doing all these things can make them stronger.

Why didn't I get him already? Why did I say he could come home with me, but I left him there? Didn't I care?

He asks me this. I don't have a good answer.

I'm his friend, the girl who saved him, but I just left him there. In a cage. Where there are sick kittens. I know that some have already died. I know Feather can smell it, the ones that are so sick and the ones that are dying.

I'm so scared for him, so sorry, that I can't stop myself from crying. For Feather and for all the pets.

I try to think about what my friends and Aunt Eira and Dom would say. Danny too. Probably. That I need to be smart and be strong. Not just sit here, crying. That doesn't help.

I wish I had my own phone, because I'd text them now, or call them. I know they'd help.

five

But I can't, so finally I make myself go get my bike and head home.

Then I think about other pets I know. Like Pixel, who is Aunt Eira's kitten. And Jayden's horse, Spirit. And Tippy, Sam's puppy. They're not trapped in a cage because they might have a horrible disease. Or catch it soon. They're all at home. Healthy and safe.

Where Feather would be now, if I'd already adopted him.

But Feather *isn't* safe.

Him knowing me hasn't been so lucky for him, after all.

I get home and Mom says I can't call Aunt Eira because she's away in New York at a conference for bloggers and Dom went with her. Sam and Jayden still aren't back from their vacations.

I go to the library, and there the librarian helps me look up pan-luke. I learn that its other name is cat distemper. It's a disease, something like the flu or pneumonia. People and dogs can't get it. Cats catch it from each other really easily. If they're adults and they've had their shots, they probably don't get it. Or they get better.

Most of the time.

But wild cats who never go to the vet easily get pan-luke. They usually don't get better. They usually die.

The way the pan-luke got in the shelter is they rescued some really tiny baby kittens from a shed. Their mother was wild, or feral. She had pan-luke and she died. Most of her kittens got it from their mother. Then other cats at the shelter got it, something like you or me catching flu from other kids at school, but more serious.

The Sunflower Pet Shelter website says they were doing everything possible to save as many of the kittens and cats as possible. The dogs were being cared for in foster homes. They thanked people for understanding and continuing to donate the things they always need like food, litter, bleach and money for medicine.

I go home to make more bracelets. It's all I know how to do that can help the pets now.

When I'm playing Candy Crush with Fairie Daisy, when I'm dusting upstairs or wrapping up the baking to take to the market or getting up or going to sleep, all I can think about is how scary it must be for everyone at the shelter. All the pets. And all the people, too.

And I cry for them.

And I try to pray.

six

It's August long weekend when Jayden gets back home. A week later, Sam is back, too and so is her Tia Margaret. Tia means aunt. Margaret is who looks after Sam because her mother is hardly ever home.

One afternoon Jayden and I are over at Sam's, out at her pool. I've thanked them again for the birthday presents and told them about my summer, the most fun parts. That was art lessons with Maudie, going to the beach, staying over at Aunt Eira's and about the guests who brought their dogs.

Eira just laughed when I showed her the bathing suit Mum got for my birthday. "I remember she had one almost like this when she was about your age," she says. "But you're right. It really doesn't suit you, does it?"

She took me to pick out a new bathing suit when we

were in the city to buy more jewellery-making supplies. She said the new bathing suit was another birthday present. Or maybe something special, now that I could finally swim again because the last stupid cast on my arm was gone.

My new bathing suit is really pretty, all turquoise. I kept the crazy colours one my Mom gave me, because Daisy loves it. It'll probably fit her in a couple of years. I already gave her the pink sunglasses and the hat.

My new swimsuit is a two-piece, easy to get on, and plain but I like it.

"What about Feather?" was almost the first thing Jayden asked me when he got home. "Do you have him yet?" So I told him about the pan-luke, and how much I miss helping out at the pet shelter. Sam asks almost the same question.

I tell them about how I've gone to the pet shelter almost every day to sit and talk to Feather. I always sit under the window near where he is. I know it's hard for him, but I think he's still not got the pan-luke. He's almost six months old now, which is like being an older teenager but almost an adult, if you're a cat.

There's a sign on the door that says the shelter is going to open up again tomorrow. I'm excited to go back.

I've already heard all about what it was like in France and Italy from Sam. She loved trying out different foods and we heard all about going to Euro Disney and all the way to the top of the Eiffel Tower in Paris.

six

She wasn't so crazy about when they met up with her father's new family in Rome, she said. Even though she hardly ever says anything about it, I know she doesn't like her Dad's new wife or being a half-sister to their daughter and two little boys. She says the girl is all right, but the boys are both total brats. But their mother just thinks everything they do is so cute and funny. And she orders Sam around, like she thinks Sam is just there to be a free babysitter.

Sam almost never loses her temper, but she says she's told her Dad to come here to visit her. She says she's never going back to his house. She says her mother thought this was great news. And then her parents had a big fight about it.

Jayden is also happy to be home. He says driving across the country with his parents, stopping in cities along the way, was interesting enough, but it just went on too long. He says when he closes his eyes, all he can see is trees and more trees and highway going by. He got bored with just sitting in the back seat playing endless video games. And he really missed riding Spirit every day.

I've told them about Danny coming to visit, and how I realize now that he never was going to come home. Getting him back to our family was just something in my mind, like a fantasy, not something that could really happen.

Him and my mom deciding they didn't want to be together any more wasn't because of anything I did. Or didn't do. Or Daisy, either. It was just an adult decision.

I guess Danny has a whole different life now, in the city. Not the one he used to have, in Seabright with Daisy, Mom and me.

I know that now.

I've told my best friends all about what happened with Julia.

But why did she do it? Hurting me. And other kids, too. We've all heard the stories about her.

"There could be lots of reasons. Stuff in her life we don't know about..." Jayden says, turning over on his lounger.

"Like what?" Sam looks doubtful. "You mean some kids might be bullies just because they're bored? Or upset about something?"

"Maybe," Jayden says. "Or there could be other reasons. Because they feel small inside and like they're not good enough."

"You think if they hurt other people, they feel like they're bigger and better?"

Jayden shrugs. "Could be. Or maybe they're jealous of other people and what they have?"

I can imagine people being jealous of Jayden and getting to be with horses and ride them any time you want. And who wouldn't want to be Sam, and live in a beautiful big house with a huge pool? I just can't imagine another kid wanting to be me, or have what I've got. What could they be jealous about? Probably not my crabby mother and annoying little sister.

"Or they just don't know any other way to behave?

That's what I think," Sam says. "Some kids just don't know good ways to get what they want or need. They only know how to use other people. Or be a bully."

"That's pretty sad," I say, considering. "You think maybe they don't even do it on purpose? I mean the bullying?"

We think about this.

"They might do it on purpose. They might think being mean is fun," Jayden says. "Or they might do it because they have a problem, like depression. Or anxiety. Or a personality disorder."

"What's that?"

"A mental illness," Sam says.

"Is there a cure for it?"

"I don't know. I guess so. Sometimes."

So maybe that's what needs to happen. That Julia get some counselling or something to figure out why she does bullying.

"I don't think it's something kids can do, on their own. I think it's an adult problem, to get help for kids that bully other people," Jayden says. "But first, to get help for the kids they hurt. That's what one of my brothers told me."

"There isn't much kids can do for her, I mean, for a bully? To change them?"

"I don't think so," Jayden says. "But I'm not sure. We could ask about that, in health class..."

We could.

What we do know is Julia will probably be back to school next week, along with everyone else. I really am not looking forward to having to see her again.

At school. Or after school, on the path home.

Or anywhere else. I know she must have some kind of problem, because she never seems happy, but I don't feel sorry for her. I don't want to help her stop bullying and act better. I don't want to do anything for her.

I don't want to forgive her.

I especially don't want to talk about it any more, even with my best friends. I just want to forget about it and have it all go away.

Eira says that won't happen. Julia being a problem for me isn't going to just go away, she says. I want her to be wrong about this.

My mother says just stay out of her way. As if that's even possible.

"So," Sam says. "Just 13 more days until middle school!"

Seems hard to believe we'll be back to school so soon. We already know it's going to be different. Better than primary.

At middle school, everybody has their own locker. Finally, I think, I have a place to keep my stuff that Daisy won't ever get into.

We'll be changing classrooms, so we don't do every subject with the same teacher. Even if you get stuck with someone like old Meanie Greenie, at least you

six

don't have them almost all day, like you do in primary school.

And there's a real cafeteria, where you can buy your lunch, like pizza or wraps or salads or pot noodles.

There're also after-school clubs, like choir and jazz band and something called the Glee Club. I haven't heard if there's an art club, or a pets club. I hope so.

Not so great news is that in middle school, you get homework. With the upstairs guests and the baking and jewellery making and volunteering at the pet shelter and keeping Daisy happy, I wonder when I'll get time to do homework.

Or anything else I want to do.

There has to be a way!

seven

"So, when the shelter is open again, you can go adopt Feather, right?" Jayden says.

"Uh, maybe. I want to. But my mom…"

"Is still saying, 'No?'"

I sigh.

"But why…?" Sam says. "For just no reason. That's so unfair!"

I really don't know why. I talked about every one of her No Pet objections in my pet presentation. I answered every single reason she has to say, "No." Every one she's said and every one I can imagine.

That was way back in June. So, she's had plenty of time to think about it. And get used to the idea of having Feather at our house. And probably she'd hardly even notice him, because he'd live in my room,

seven

mine and Daisy's. I'd do all the looking after him.

"We could adopt Feather ourselves," Sam says, as if she's thinking out loud.

"Kids can't," I say. "It has to be your parent or guardian. They have to sign some papers. And promise you'll be a good pet parent."

"What if we asked Margaret to adopt Feather? She could just give him to you?" Margaret is Sam's family's housekeeper and cook. She's always been kind to me and Jayden and to all Sam's friends. I know Sam loves her as much as I love Aunt Eira.

"It still won't work, even if Margaret agrees, because cats have a microchip with the owner's name and address and phone number on it."

"Oh yeah," Sam says. "I guess I knew that. Tippy has a microchip, too."

"And it wouldn't really be honest, would it?" Jayden says. "Even if Margaret agreed to do it."

We all think about this.

"What about your aunt?"

"She says she doesn't set the rules in our house. And I just have to convince Mum…"

"But your mother doesn't want to be convinced, does she? For some reason you don't know about and can't guess."

This is true.

"Maybe it's just because your mom's going to have a baby?"

"But why would that matter?"

"Well," Jayden says, "There's this crazy old belief that cats can make babies sick. Or even kill them. It's all nonsense, my mom says, but some people still believe it."

"Sounds really dumb," Sam says. "Why would a cat want to hurt a baby?"

I agree. "It must just be people who don't know cats because they've never had one."

"Like your family?" Jayden says. "Oh, sorry...didn't mean to..."

But he's right. Maybe my mom is just saying no because it's something different. Having a cat is something we've never done before.

It's a change. Like living without Danny. Or starting the cookie business. Or selling jewellery. Or starting middle school.

Doing something differently is always hard and scary, until you start. That's what Dom says. He says, "You just have to plunge right in and do it!"

"So, you were talking about Danny, but did you find out any more about your real father?" Sam gets up to pour out the last of the lemonade into our glasses.

"Not much, really," I say, and tell them, "His first name is Malcolm. He lives in Ireland, or he used to live there. I don't know anything else about him, or how he met my mom."

"I've wondered that sometimes. How my parents ever got together," Jayden says.

seven

"Me too," Sam says. "But I guess it's their business, if they don't want to tell people. I mean their kids."

But is it? Wouldn't that help you know a lot, to know why your parents got together? And if they were excited and happy to have you? Wouldn't that be a happy story you'd want to hear and a fun story for them to tell?

......

Even though it's a really hot day, Jayden still has his tee shirt on over his swim trunks. It's still wet, because he never takes it off. Maybe because he doesn't like how his chest looks. Or he thinks he needs to have more muscles.

Or he just doesn't want to get sunburn.

"Hey, did your mom decide to get your family a computer yet?" This is another question I was hoping they wouldn't ask. We've already been told that we should have a laptop or desk computer to do our homework. I also know there were only three kids in my class last year who didn't. Everyone feels sorry for them.

"Um...no..." I see the same pitying looks from Sam and Jayden. They both have their own computers and their own phones. It's only the really poor kids who don't.

My mother is still saying no child needs a computer or a phone, because that's just asking for trouble. And that all kids do is goof off and text each other when they're supposed to be learning things in school. Or they're online, where she says there are a lot of trolls and lurkers. They're evil people who try to hurt kids.

I've tried to tell her that a computer or a phone is just like any other technology. You have to learn how to use it and stay safe. And we do learn that, at school. We've had lessons about computers ever since grade 3. And we did a whole unit about staying safe online in grade 4 and another one in grade 5. I know what cyberbullying is, and about how you don't put personal information about yourself online, like your home address.

I bet we'll still be learning more about using phones and computers properly and staying safe in middle school.

I said phones and computers are only dangerous when you don't know how to use them. Like driving a car, or using a knife, or cooking on the stove, or riding a motorcycle. Nobody would use those things without learning how first. But my mother says she's an adult, so she knows better.

She just doesn't listen.

At least not to me.

And I don't know how I can change that.

……

The pet shelter finally re-opens on the last weekend of summer.

seven

I already know Feather is OK. He's told me so.

Jayden's mom also phoned and told me, after Jayden told her how worried I was about Feather.

For a thank you gift, I made her a pet portrait of Jayden and his brother, Patrick, riding their horses. She said she'd hang it up in her vet clinic. That might get more people calling me, wanting pet portraits.

What an amazing idea!

The pan-luke meant some kittens did die, and that makes me so sad. But almost all the cats and most of the kittens are saved.

I'm so happy to be able to see them all again and to cuddle with them. Especially with Feather.

He's still pretty grumpy about why I can't take him home.

I don't blame him. It makes me sad and angry, too. How can I explain to him that I keep asking my mother, but she just won't listen?

There's a happy surprise at the shelter. The director, Ms. Valour, says she's noticed how hard I work when I'm there. She said that she and the Board of Directors, they're all the bosses, decided that maybe kids like me CAN be volunteers.

And she said the Directors want to meet me. They have some questions, she said, about what they call "reaching out to more young people to contribute." That means finding more kids that want to help out at the shelter, I guess.

I try to think about who that could be. And how I'd

find them. Because, when I think about it, they'd be kids I'd like to know!

eight

"Welcome to Grade 6 and Welcome to Middle School" it says on the whiteboard, in coloured-in letters so big it takes up all the space across the front of the classroom.

I've never had a man teacher before. I'm wondering what it will be like, even though Jayden has told us he's a good guy. Mr. Cadeau was Jayden's teacher for grade five and now we've got him for home room in grade six. Home room is always the first class and the last class every day.

Mr. Cadeau looks pretty cool in skinny jeans and a black tee shirt. His curly hair is sort of long-ish. He looks really young but he must be a grown-up, because you have to be to get a job as a school teacher. He reminds me of Jayden's brother Patrick.

This is going to be interesting.

There are three grade 6s at Evangeline Middle School, so there's only five kids from my old school in this class, plus a lot of kids I don't know from other primary schools, the ones who come from Minas Inlet and Curry's Corner and Woodland Bay and Upper Canard. Those are all little towns near here. But luckily Sam and Jayden are in my homeroom, so we'll always start the day together.

"Now, you might all be wondering what's going to happen in our time together in Grade 6," Mr. Cadeau is saying. "Uh, Hunter, turn off the phone and put it away, please. Now, what's Grade 6 really all about?"

"Goofing off," somebody says. Most of the kids laugh.

"Nice try, but no. Anyone else know?"

"How to eat lunch," one of the boys in the back shouts. Just about everybody laughs.

He smiles. "Let's hope you've already learnt that. Grade 6 is about some things you've already been studying at school, like math, science, music, communication arts, history, art, health and physical education. And there are some new subjects, like learning a language that might be new to you such as French or Spanish or German, computer coding and personal finance. That means being smart about your money. All this is absolutely true…"

Kids groan. "Yep, that's the news, we're all going to be working hard, because there's a lot of good stuff to discover and explore in grade 6 and throughout your middle school careers. That means this year and then in grades 7 and 8.

"BUT - and this is a big fat but, by the way…" lots of kids giggle when he says this, "there are three things

eight

you each MUST learn in middle school. Can anyone tell me what one of these things is?

"How to skip class," someone says.

"How to get out of doing homework," another kid says.

"Very funny, but enough joking around," he says. "There are three serious things it is your responsibility to learn in your middle school years. These three things are…" and he clicks on his laptop and a slide image appears on the wall.

"ONE, your bodies are changing."

"Yeah, girls get boobies. We already know that!" a boy says.

Mr. Cadeau says, "Both boys' bodies and girls' bodies change, in many important ways. Your bodies are going to feel different and they're going to work a bit differently than you're used to.

"The second big topic you each need to learn is how to get used to and understand your changing brain. Because, just like your body, your brain is changing and leaving childhood behind."

He gives us a serious look. "You no longer have a child body and you no longer have a child brain."

"Oh yeah?" that same boy says. "I do!"

"But not for much longer, Tony," our teacher says. "Now, can anyone guess what number THREE serious topic might be? Or does anyone know?"

"What we're going to do when we grow up?" That's a

girl I recognize because she bought a bracelet a few weeks ago at the Saturday Market. I look to see if she's wearing it. She is.

"Hmm, I'd like to say you're close, Meredith, but no points for that one. Any other suggestions?" he waits a moment.

"No one going to take a stab at what's behind Door Number Three?"

No one says anything.

"It's this. You have to figure out who you really are. Not who your parents want you to be. Not who your friends want you to be. Not just like your big brother or sister or someone else you know. Not just like some rock star or actor on TV.

"You have to figure out who YOU are. Anyone know what this is called?"

"Identity," Jayden says.

"And that means…?"

"Knowing who you really are. Inside."

"Exactly, Jayden. Thank you," Mr. Cadeau says. "See you all again later today," as the bell goes off and we start to gather up our stuff and file out to go to the next class. For me and Sam, that's girls' gym where we have to play floor hockey. For Jayden, boy's gym means football practice. I know he hates it.

But, like us having to learn how to do indoor sports, which I think is pointless and stupid, there's no choice. Everybody has to take gym class until high school.

eight

I wonder if by then we'll all know about our brains and bodies and, most of all, who we really are because we learned it in Grade 6.

Jayden decides to join Junior Choir, as an after-school club. Sam says she wants nothing to do with joining band. Her mother already makes her practice five hours a day. Three on piano and two on violin. She'd like to join something, she says, but she doesn't know what. And she probably doesn't have time for it, anyways. All Evangeline School has for the grade 6s is band, choir, tennis club and drama club. They put on plays.

None of those sound very exciting to Sam. Me, either. But I have another idea for a club. First, I have to get permission to start it. Not from my mom. From the school. Probably from the principal, but I don't know who it is you're supposed to ask.

When I stay after school one day to talk to Mr. Cadeau, he says he thinks a pet club is a great idea and he'd be happy to be the club's sponsor, if I get permission to start it. He says every club has to have a teacher be the sponsor. That means they're in charge.

He says it's the principal who gets to decide about if we can start a new club. I'm pretty surprised to find out that the principal is Mr. Maclean. But he's away right now, so the vice-principal, Ms. Vida, is who I need to ask.

So, right after school the next day, I head for the office with my plan about what a pet club would be like. And I know, when I get home, Mom is going to ask why I'm late and I'm going to say because I had to go see the principal. And she's going to say, "Oh, Lord. What is it this time?"

And that is just what she says, but not about me going to see the principal, because when I get home there's a police car parked in our driveway.

"Morley, in here," Mom calls.

I groan, wondering what sort of trouble I might be in this time.

But it isn't about me. It's about Julia and also about the renters. The ones who threw Feather off our balcony.

The officer tells us that they have decided not to go ahead with their investigation, because Julia is 12, but she's never been in trouble with the police before, so she isn't going to be charged. That is, if my mother and I agree.

I don't want to. I think she should have to answer for what she did to me and to other kids. I don't want her to just pretend it meant nothing to hurt kids and trash their stuff. And keep doing it.

My mother says, no, she should get another chance to improve her behaviour. The police officer nods.

I guess what I want doesn't count.

As long as Julia gets counselling and completes 20 hours of community service, Constable Levy says, the charges will be dropped. Mom says she'll explain it all to me.

Later, she says that yes, Julia hurt people including

eight

me, but that now that's going to end. And I've just about healed, haven't I? The bruises are pretty much greenish yellow now, not black or blue any more.

She says that community service means doing volunteer work, like helping out at the food bank or visiting very elderly people or helping out at the pet shelter, like I do. That's the one I really hope Julia, or her Dad, don't choose for her 20 hours of community service.

That's all she has to do. Volunteer for 20 hours. I've spent way more time than that volunteering at Sunflower Pet Shelter, and I didn't even have to be ordered to do it. It's not fair!

The other thing Constable Levy has come to tell us is that they did find the renters who used to live upstairs. They totally trashed our home and stole money and other things from us and didn't pay their rent. Then they just left, and we had to clean up the mess. But that's also when Mom changed the upstairs of our house, from an apartment to rent into Bed and Breakfast rooms for tourists.

The renter man and woman have been arrested. Constable Levy doesn't say what happened to their baby. But we know what happened to their kitten. That was Feather.

"And what about the rent money?" my mother asks. "And everything they stole from us? My grandmother's candlesticks? And the damage they did...?"

The constable looks sad. "Not much chance of getting anything from them, I'm afraid, ma'am," he says. "When we apprehended them, they didn't have much more than their clothes and phones. But you will have your insurance…"

"So that's it? They just get away with stealing from me?"

"You're likely best rid of them, Ms. Star," he says. "And it's all very sad for them too, I'd imagine. They've lost their little girl…"

A shocked look crosses my mother's face. She turns away to hide it. I wonder if the policeman noticed. Maybe not. He doesn't know my mother like I do.

"There are some resources for victims of crime, like counselling…I could give you a name of someone…" he says.

Mom dismisses this idea with a wave of her hand. "We don't need that."

He finishes his tea and thanks us and then he's gone.

"So that's that," Mom says. "I guess you live and learn…"

Learn what, I wonder. To do a better job of hiding your money?

Not to let thieves live in your house?

Mom isn't in the mood to explain.

But I do find out that the insurance will pay back the money from the pet donations that the renters stole. Most of it. As well as help pay for all the renovations upstairs that made it nice again so we could have the guests.

I also know that we get way more money having

eight

guests than when we had renters. When they paid the rent, that is. So maybe you could say, in that way, those awful renter people did us a favor.

For the rest of the missing pet money, I'll just have to keep selling more bracelets to make it up. I already knew that.

Summer is ending, even though it's still pretty hot out.

We still have lots of guests, but now they're just about all older people, like my grandparents. Gramps and Margie have written to say they'll be home from their latest cruise and so they'll be with us for Thanksgiving. They say not to worry about a thing, they'll be fine with just a simple Thanksgiving with their darling daughters and grand-children. That means Daisy and me and also our cousins, Aunt Sorcha's little boys.

My mom doesn't look too pleased to hear this, even though I know she gets on with Margie good enough.

Our real grandmother died long ago, before I was born. All I know about that is she was smoking in bed and fell asleep and a fire started. Mom doesn't ever say much about her. Now Gramps is married to Margie. She's OK. And Gramps is a hoot, especially when he pulls out his accordion. He likes to make up silly songs.

Mom's doing less of the work at home and less baking than she did. Her baking helper is doing more of the work. And sometimes she also helps me with doing the guest rooms, because Aimee, our summer helper, has gone back to high school.

Mom takes a long nap every afternoon. But not for much longer, she says. Our new brother or sister should be here before Christmas.

She didn't go back to her school secretary job. Instead, she started parent leave, which she says means she'll be home until next summer. Then maybe she'll get another job. But we don't need to worry about that, because we have the guests and the baking business doing so well.

She's still doing the baking, but now she has Sheila to help her. Sheila isn't very much older than me, but she has a baby and she had to leave high school and work, Mom says, to support them. I like Sheila. And she's really, really good at making cakes and cookies. Almost as good as Mom is.

Aunt Eira and I are the ones who sell our baking and bracelets at the Saturday market. Eira says this is just another way to help my mom. And some days, it's Sheila who helps me sell at the market, while Eira and Dom babysit Daisy and Amélie. That's Sheila's baby.

Even Daisy pitches in sometimes at our market booth, helping put cookies in the bags. She's especially good at looking sweet and saying thank you to the customers and, of course, they just love her.

I've noticed when Daisy wears a lot of bracelets, people notice and we sell even more bracelets than when she doesn't come to market with us.

Not long after school starts again, a really incredible thing happens. All of a sudden, Mom says I can adopt Lucky Feather.

eight

I have no idea why she changed her mind, but maybe it doesn't matter. I'm so excited, I can hardly wait. I want to go to the shelter RIGHT AWAY. Mum thinks this is really funny. Or maybe she's just happy because getting Feather would make me so happy.

We can go get him right after school, she says.

But I couldn't because that day was the first meeting of the new Pet Club. It was my idea. I had to be there!

Mr. Maclean still isn't back to being our principal. There's a rumour going around that it's because he's sending Julia to a different school. One of the ones where kids live at the school. If that's true my Julia problem will be solved. I'll never have to see her.

I was hoping so. Maybe at that fancy school they'd figure out how to make her stop bullying people and be a nicer person. That would be good, just in case she ever came home for vacations from her new school. And, I guess, also good for the other kids at that school.

Ms. Vida, the vice-principal, said she thought a club about having pets and helping pets at the shelter is a really good idea. So now there are 10 kids who are going to meet in Mr. Cadeau's room every Monday and Thursday after school. That's how many signed up for the new pet club.

He says it's a wonderful idea for kids to get involved and learn kindness, compassion and empathy.

He says he's proud of me, for being thoughtful and creative, and what he calls "a natural leader."

And, he says, when I finally, finally, get my Feather, I

can bring him to Pet Club and introduce him to everyone. And talk about the Get A Pet project I did last year.

And the good work pet shelters do to save animals like him.

I've got everything ready for Feather to come home. To me and his forever home. I set up the litter box and filled it with fresh litter. I got out his water bowl and food bowl and washed them. I put his pet bed right next to mine. All his toys are in a little basket on the lowest shelf of my bookcase where he can get them.

I know what vet we'll be going to. That's Jayden's mum, Dr. Van Haan. We have her clinic's number next to the landline phone, for emergencies. And I've memorized it.

I am really, *really* ready to have a pet cat join our family.

"You know, Morley, I expect you to do everything this pet needs..." Mom says.

I do know. Like scoop the poop. And feed him. Put fresh water in his bowl every day. Check his ears and teeth. Brush his coat. Notice if he seems to be sick and take him to the vet.

"And not just when you feel like it..."

And help pay for him, Mom reminds me. But I'm not worried about that part at all. I have more than enough money, from selling bracelets and doing pet portraits for people. Even after I give half the profit I make to the Sunflower Pet Shelter as a donation to

eight

help the pets every month, I've still got enough money to have Feather.

When we get to the shelter, Mom stops to chat with Shanelle, who's the one on the front desk today. But I say a quick, "Hi Shani," and run back to Room B. And Feather's cage.

But it's empty.

Maybe he's in the cat playroom?

But no. There are cats sleeping in there. And playing. And giving themselves a cat bath. But no Feather.

And I can't hear him in my head. I've been calling him, saying *I'm coming, I'm finally coming Feather, I'm here for you. We're going home!*

But there's no reply.

His cage is empty. He's not in the cat play area. He's not in the back.

He's not here.

"Feather!" I cry, racing back to the front. "Feather. Where is he?"

"Feather?" Shanelle says. "I don't think..."

"Black and white, with gold-green eyes. A boy. He's about six months old. And..."

"OK." She says. "Slow down. Now, what's his name here at the shelter? I'll look..."

I tell her. Shane. A stupid name. I think names should have a meaning. They should say something about who you are. Shane is nothing sort of name. It doesn't say anything about who he is.

I wait and wait, wishing I could rush around the desk and just look on her computer. I could probably make it work faster than Shanelle can.

"Oh...uh. Yes. Shane already got adopted. Sorry."

nine

"WHAT? THAT CAN'T BE TRUE!"

"Morley!" my mother says. "Calm down!"

"Someone else? Someone took him? But he was supposed to come home with me. I PROMISED him...!"

I feel like I'm choking. Or like I'm going to throw up. Or like there is a gigantic scream inside of me that needs to come out. "But how? When?"

"Yeah," Shani says. "Says here it was yesterday. Someone came in. This old guy. Said he needed a good mouser and he didn't mind taking a black cat. Even though they're bad luck...which is lucky for us, I guess. Because usually people don't want black pets..."

I can't believe it. Feather, gone to someone else's home.

To be someone else's pet.

To sit in their front window, watching for them to

come home.

Or sit in their lap, when they're reading or painting or doing crafts or...just sitting and dreaming.

To curl up in bed with them, when they don't feel well. Or they're just going to sleep.

To be their best friend.

Forever.

"He's got this workshop and he said he needed a cat to..." She turns away to answer the phone.

I feel like I'm going to explode.

"Who?" I say, when she finally gets off the phone. "Who was it? This man..."

"Sorry. We have a rule to never reveal any information about adopters," Shani says with a sniff. "But we do have other pets in need...why don't you go look?"

I already know that. I already know all the cats waiting in Room A. And Room B. I've changed their water. Filled their food dishes. Cleaned their litter boxes. Brushed their coats. Cuddled them.

Feather is the one I want. And need. And don't want to live without.

"Well, Morley, I guess we just waited too long," my mother says. "But you can..."

Suddenly, I can't see anything and realize I'm crying. I don't know what to do next. I don't know if I should scream or howl or curl up in a ball on the floor or run out the door and never come back.

nine

"Oh, really, Morley, stop this childish carrying on," my mother says, grabbing me by the shoulder. "You're causing a scene and embarrassing both of us, over nothing. I've said you can have a cat. Just go back there and pick one! They're all pretty much the same. They all need a home..."

She goes back to chatting with Shani.

I stumble outside and get in our car. I send out a message to Feather in my head.

Feather, where are you? Where? It's Morley. Tell me. I'll come for you...

But there is only the *shush-shush* of the wind in the maple trees, the ones that are turning to orangey-gold. Like they always do, this time of year.

I'm alone in my head.

Feather isn't there.

Mom gets in the car and says, "I thought you wanted a cat. So, I don't see the problem...?"

"This is your fault!" I shout at her. Then I clam up and refuse to talk to her all the way home. She just turns on the radio and ignores me.

Sam says, "We'll find him. I'll help. I know Jayden will, too. Let's make a plan for how we'll do it."

Aunt Eira says. "It's just too bad. After you planned on having Feather for so long. Darling, I know you must be so disappointed..."

Mom says there's lots of other good pets. I should pick out a different cat. If I still want one. Or a kitten, if I want. Or a dog. But not a big dog, because she doesn't want to be out in our garden scooping poop from a big dog. And they eat more, so they cost more.

Daisy hears this and says she wants a dog. "Yes, I think that's a good idea," Mom says.

And how unfair is that? I wanted a pet for so long and did so much to show my mother I'd be a responsible pet owner. And she always said no. But Daisy just says she thinks she wants a dog and doesn't even have to do anything to get her pet and Mom says, "Yes."

Just like that!

It just makes me so mad that I say things that maybe I shouldn't have. But my mouth was working before my brain did.

Like how unfair Mom always is.

That Daisy always gets anything she wants. While I have to work so hard for it.

And what I really want to say, but don't, that she likes Daisy but, for some reason, she doesn't like me.

"Morley, I've told you, ENOUGH!" my mother shouts. "I just can't take all this grief from you, especially not now. I've told you, stress is really dangerous for the baby. And me!" And she rubs her huge belly.

"So, act your age for once. Go to your room until you're ready to come out and be a reasonable person and stop always insisting on having your own way!"

"Really?" I say. "You mean, just like you? Because it's always ONLY what you want. ONLY your way. Like

nine

you're the only person who lives here. The only person who matters!"

But I go. Because I'm so angry with her and with Daisy and so sad about missing Feather I think I'm going to curl up into a little ball like a bomb and explode.

I think about calling Danny, or maybe sending him an e-mail from Aunt Eira's computer. But what could he do? I can't imagine a single thing he could do now that would help. That is, if he even wants to.

"So," Jayden says. "We've got to find Feather. And convince the man that's got him to let you have him."

We're in the lunch room, munching on today's special, vegetarian lasagna. It just tastes like ordinary pasta with ordinary tomato sauce and hardly any cheese. I don't really like it, but the only other thing they have is turkey nuggets and they're even worse.

"That's two plans," Sam says, taking some kimchi with her gold and red chopsticks. It stinks, and other kids tease her about eating it. But she says it's not so bad, once you get used to it. The kimchi, I think she means, not the teasing.

Sam is half Korean, so kids pick on her about being different. She mostly ignores it. I've hardly ever seen her get mad. She doesn't have a temper, like me. It's like she just floats above any mean thing other kids say.

"Two plans...one is how to find a pet cat that might be an inside cat that nobody ever sees unless, maybe, they sit in a window."

I smile. I know how to find an inside cat. At least one special one. But I won't tell even my two best friends that I know what Feather is thinking and how he feels, inside my head. And I know he can hear me, when I call him, in my thoughts. They'd think I'm nuts.

It would be even worse if other kids found out. Like horrible Julia.

Or one of Julia's mean-girl friends or some other bully in our school, because Julia isn't the only one. They would use that information to torture me forever.

"So what's the second plan?" Jayden says. "I think I know. It's once you find Feather, how are you going to talk the owner into giving him to you?"

We think about this. Two tough problems.

"First we have to find him," I say. "Then, figure out what to say to get him back."

I'd like to just rush in and steal him. But even though I want Feather so much, that's just not right. If I did that, I'd be no different than those awful renter people we used to have living upstairs who stole from our family.

After school, before school, on weekends, any time there is, I go searching for Lucky Feather. Sometimes walking, sometimes on my bike.

Always staying on streets or sidewalks of the busier streets and never using the walking trail where there are less people around, but that's where Julia attacked me.

Sometimes Aunt Eira or Dom drives me around.

nine

They've also helped by putting up signs all over our town that say:

HAVE **YOU**

SEEN

FEATHER?

Reward offered.

Contact Eira Star

And it also has Eira's phone number and e-mail address.

On Saturdays, I sell bracelets and cookies and squares and have the poster up in our booth. Lots of people stop to chat and say kind things, even some of the kids and teachers from school and Ms. Vida. But nobody remembers seeing Feather. Or the man that just adopted him.

I make more bracelets.

I go to pet club and tell kids how to do their own Get A Pet project.

I try out some fancy silver wire bracelets and earrings with sea glass or turquoise and amber for Eira to sell on her website. I help bake and draw and write and play with Daisy and take swimming lessons. I ride horses with Jayden and hang out with Sam. I do all the usual Morley stuff.

And the whole time, I think and think about Feather.

And search for him.

And call out to him in my head, while I walk up and down every single street in our town. And then in the other towns nearby, like Port Williams and Canning and Canard and Scot's Bay. And along all the roads in between.

Sometimes Mom helps me look, but that's only once or twice. She's got two baking helpers now. They're women who, mom says, just need a lucky break in life. Or a second chance. I think that means they just need a job because they have a kid and no husband. Like our family.

Getting a second chance is something I think about, while I'm searching for Feather. How you can make a mistake, and then get a second chance? That's what I need. With Feather.

But do I deserve it? I don't know.

I keep looking and looking and wishing for my lucky break that will help me find Feather. Sometimes Aunt Eira drives me to look. Or Dom. And one time, Aunt Sorcha does.

I get really tired, but I never think that I should just give up. Because I KNOW Feather is meant to come home to us, the Star family.

I know he's meant to be my little cat.

And I'm meant to be his girl.

I'm confident I can find him. For my secret reason, but also because look at all the things I already found this year. Or figured out. Or found out.

nine

Like how to make bracelets.

And how to do watercolour painting. I learned that from Maudie Lewis this summer.

And how to sell things to people at the market.

And how to do a project and make it into a presentation.

And how to look after pets.

And how to find out things you need to know on the Internet.

I learned how to start a business and how to know how much money it costs to make a bracelet and how much to charge people for it, so you make a profit.

And how to start a club.

And how to be a volunteer and help raise money for a charity.

And how to get better, when you've been hurt bad.

Just thinking about all these things I learned makes me feel strong. It helps me be confident. I know I can do anything I work at and really try to get good at. Even when bad things happen.

ten

I feel like I'm getting so good at knowing all the streets of our town and the towns near us, I could be a tour guide. If I was old enough to drive a car, I'd already know where everything is around here.

Then, one day when I'm not even searching for Feather is the day that I find him.

Mom says we have to go over to Mr. Maclean's house that afternoon, right after school. She says he and Julia just got back from looking at new schools for her, because she needs a fresh start.

Also, Julia has something particular to say to me. If it's her doing a fake apology, I don't even want to hear it. I don't believe she'd really feel sorry for all the times she called me names, or bumped up against me really hard, or did threats, or hit me, or other ugly stuff to hurt me.

Stuff that still hurts, even now that the bruises are mostly gone. Because it hurts me in my heart. And in

ten

my head.

But mom says everyone makes mistakes sometimes. We all do, she says, because we're human. And when we make mistakes, we need to apologize. And make amends. That means try to undo the harm. As if that's even possible, with someone like Julia. There isn't any eraser for cruelty and violence, is there?

She can't undo all the horrible things she's done. Even if she really wants to.

I just can't imagine anything Julia will do. Or could do. To make it better.

To act better.

If Mr. Maclean makes Julia apologize, Mom is going to make me say, "Hey, that's OK, it was nothing." Which is a big fat lie. It was not nothing.

I try to tell mom this. She says I'm being obstinate and stubborn and as mean-spirited towards Julia as she was to me. And to get over myself and try to think of poor Julia, whose mother died when she was a young girl. And how lucky I am not to ever have gone through such a horrible thing.

I say, "Sure. But she didn't lose her father, did she?"

Mom doesn't say anything to that. She just turns up the radio and drives.

So, we go over to Mr. Maclean's and Julia's house. I don't even want to get out of the car, but Mom makes me come into their house. It's neat enough, but everything is beige. And it smells funny, like some kind of air-freshener.

Julia is slouched on a chair in the living room. She's scowling. "Julia went to the counselors," Mr. Maclean explains when we're all sitting down. "She sees what she did was hurtful and wrong."

Julia just sits there, not looking at anyone. I can tell she doesn't even care one bit.

"So now, she wants to apologize to you, Morley," Mr. Maclean says. "And also ask what she can do to make amends. That means, to make it up to you?"

Nothing, I think. I don't want her apology. I don't want to shake her hand, or just hug and say let's be friends. I don't want to waste any time on her.

And I really, really don't want to be here.

"So, Julia, tell Morley what you have to say," Mr. Maclean says.

"Yeah. Whatever." Julia says.

Mr. Maclean looks annoyed, but his voice is still the same, strong but kindly.

Julia is fiddling with her phone.

"Julia, that's not good enough."

"Sure, sorry, yada, yada, yada." Julia says. "It was all just a joke anyways. Nothing really happened."

"A joke? A joke? Beating up a smaller girl till she's black and blue is a joke?" my mother says, putting down her coffee cup and taking my side for a change. She heaves herself up from the couch. "I don't think so. And that's no kind of sincere apology, is it Julia? I don't think you have one bit of regret about what you

ten

did, hurting other people. Come on, Morley…"

"A big fat joke!" Julia says, smiling for the first time. "HA ha ha!"

"Oh, Julia," Mr. Maclean says.

Mom grabs her handbag and fishes around for the keys. "Morley, I think we're done here," she says, giving Mr. Maclean her angry look.

I wonder if she's finally going to realize that Julia is a bully. That's all she is and all she knows how to do. Her dad, Mr. Maclean, doesn't care. Or he doesn't even notice what she does. Or he doesn't know what to do to make her stop.

The further I can get away from her – from both of them - the better.

We go out to the car. Mr. Maclean doesn't even try to follow us and apologize.

But here's the crazy thing. That was the day I finally found Feather. And it was all because we went to stupid Julia's house.

eleven

I know it's hard to believe, but it's the truth. I don't think I would have found Feather if it wasn't for us going to the Maclean's house that day.

Not that bully Julia helped me on purpose. She didn't.

And wouldn't.

Here's how it happened.

I was going around to get in the car when I heard it. Just a little faint meow.

Just one.

I'd know it anywhere.

It was coming from a sort of barn, or maybe it was a big garage, behind the house next door to the Maclean's house. I'd walked down this street before, looking for Feather, but I guess out on the sidewalk

eleven

was just too far away from the workshop-garage place for me to hear him in my head.

But we were parked in the Maclean's driveway. That was much closer to their neighbour's back yard.

I didn't tell Mom this.

All the way home, she was going on and on about how hard it must be for poor Mr. Maclean, raising a daughter alone, and such a miserable ungrateful girl with such poor manners.

Just proof, she said, that Mr. Maclean should have remarried after his wife died, because that girl absolutely needs a mother.

How she'd read about girls and bullying and it's just so hard to stop it.

"Especially when their parent doesn't even see what they're doing and isn't even trying to stop it," I say. "Or maybe he is, but it isn't working."

"We can't know that, Morley," Mom says. "Maybe he's doing everything he can. Everything he knows how to do."

It sounded like Mom was feeling sorry for Mr. Maclean.

I wasn't. "And he's a school principal. So you think he'd know about things like that."

Mom just nods.

"What Julia did and said, when she was supposed to be apologizing to me was really just more bullying, wasn't it?"

"Well, yes. Yes it was," Mom says. "But..."

"She was trying to make me feel small and weak and like I don't matter. That's bullying. It's how bullies work. They try to tear you down and make you feel small. Like nothing. They try to totally trash your self-confidence. We talked about it in Mr. Cadeau's class."

"Maybe it's because she feels small and like nothing herself," Mom says. "Though I'm not making excuses for her, Morley. There is no excuse for hurting others. None. She should have apologized. And she needs to change her ways. Maybe this new school will help her learn some better ways to deal with people."

For once, Mom and I agree about something.

As soon as I get home, I wait until Mom isn't anywhere near our phone, so she won't hear what I have to say to Aunt Eira.

Then I call my aunt and ask her to pick me up after school tomorrow. I say I have something exciting to tell her. And I need her help. I'm so relieved when she says, "Yes."

If there's anyone who can be charming and talk to the man who has Feather and get him to say he'll give him to us, it's my Aunt Eira. I can't wait to see what she says to the man who has my cat.

My future cat. Soon to be my right-now cat. My all-the-time cat.

My forever cat.

I just know it.

Because I have a plan.

twelve

The next day, Aunt Eira and I knock on the front door of the house next to the Maclean's house.

No one answers.

Then we try the side door.

Still no answer. Even though there's a car in the driveway.

Hungry, Feather says. *Girl, I need food. Girl, help me!*

"Well," Eira says, "we tried. We'll come back another time."

But I'm already running around back to the workshop. There's smoke coming out the chimney. It smells like an apple wood fire. Or maybe cherry wood. I love that smell.

Feather says he's just seen a mouse and he's chasing it, but he doesn't know how to kill it. Even though he's so hungry. That's probably because his mother didn't teach him, I tell him in my head.

How to kill a mouse is one of the things a queen – that's the name for a mother cat – always teaches her kittens. Unless she dies when they're still so tiny they don't learn how to hunt for their own food.

I know that's probably what happened to Feather and his brothers and sisters. I don't know how those upstairs renter people got him when he was still too young to leave his mother. I ask Feather about this, but he doesn't remember.

Cats know how to stalk something, from instinct. That means they're born knowing how to do it. They also know how to pounce. But, just like people, there's a lot they aren't born already knowing, like how to jump and how to climb stairs. They have to learn.

Feather hasn't learnt how to get mice so he'll survive. He's starving. I really have no idea how to teach him to kill mice. Maybe that's something only his mother could do.

"I really don't know if…" Eira's saying as she catches up to me at the workshop door. But I'm already knocking again. Finally, a man with a lot of shaggy white hair, a beard and a grubby old sweater and baggy pants opens the door. He seems surprised to see us.

He looks kind of like a cranky Santa Claus, except his clothes aren't red. They're kind of no colour, like he put them in the washing machine with bleach too many times. And they have no shape. So you can't tell if he's fat or skinny.

He doesn't look friendly.

twelve

I try to look around him to see if I can spot Feather.

"Hello," Aunt Eira says. "This is my niece, Morley and I'm Eira Star and you are...?"

The man kind of grunts. "Noble," he says. "Noble Ferguson. Folks call me Gus. But I'm not buying any of whatever it is you're sellin'."

"Um. Yes. Mr. Ferguson. Gus. We heard you adopted a cat recently?"

He nods. Listening, but not smiling.

"Was it a black cat, by any chance?" Aunt Eira says in her smiley voice. "Quite young, still? With gold-green eyes? White paws?"

"Maybe," the man says.

Hungry! Feather says. *Girl, help me. Can't get mouse. Want food.*

"Could you tell me why you chose that particular cat?"

"Is this some sort of survey or something?," Gus says, sounding grumpy and like he wants to get back to whatever he was doing. "I told the shelter people everything they wanted to know. And I paid them. And I think that's all I hafta do, isn't it?"

"Yes, Mr. Ferg...uh, Gus, it is. Absolutely. But, you see, my niece was hoping to adopt the same cat. She came to get him, and..."

"But I got there first," the man says. "And now you come around here thinking I'll just hand over the cat because your little girl wants it? No, I don't think so. And I've got work to do, so good day to you both," he says and shuts the door.

Feather, I say. *I'll be back. Real soon. I'll bring food for you. I promise.*

"That went well," my aunt says when we get back to her car. I think she's probably being sarcastic. "But don't worry, I have another idea. We'll wear him down."

"Feather was hungry," I say. "That man didn't feed him any cat food. Isn't that cruelty to animals?"

"How do you know?" Eira asks. "He didn't invite us in, so we didn't look everywhere. There might have been a food bowl somewhere we couldn't see from just standing at the door."

Because I know. Because Feather said so. I know cats can survive for longer than people without food, even without water. But not for days and days. They have to eat. Just like we do.

Feather knows there are mice. He can smell them and hear them. He can catch them. But that's all he can do.

I have to get back here, really soon, with food for him. Or he could starve to death.

"So, what do you think we could do?" Aunt Eira asks. We're back at her house, having what she calls a pet strategy session. "What's Plan B?"

"We could give that man, uh, Gus, money to buy Feather from him," I say. "I've got enough…"

"What if he says, "No way!"

twelve

"We could adopt another cat for him and just trade."

"But what about the microchip? It all has to be registered. All the cats from the pet shelter are microchipped." I know a microchip is a tiny little disc, like a memory stick only really small, put just under the skin at the back of a pet's neck. It doesn't hurt them. And it works better than them wearing a collar and tags, in case they get lost.

"We could sneak in and steal him."

"Hmm. Tempting. But no."

"OK," I say. "I give up. What do you think we should do?"

"Let's sleep on it," Aunt Eira says. "Let your brain work on the problem overnight. Lots of times you wake up the next morning with the answer!"

But what I wake up with next morning is a headache. A really bad one, because I couldn't sleep. All night, I kept worrying and worrying about Feather. Then about other things like what if people stop buying the bracelets and other jewellery I make, so I don't have enough money to buy all the things Feather needs, like food and visits to the vet?

And what if Julia comes back to our school and what if she's really mad because she thinks I told on her? I don't know how to stop her beating me up.

And what if the guests stop coming, the ones who want to stay in our upstairs?

What if people stop buying cookies and mom has to find another job right away?

And what about my father? My real father. Why isn't he here with us? Or at least he could come to visit, like Danny does. I've started the Find My Father Project. I'm doing some drawings about what our home is like and a notebook about my life. Writing about who I am. Sort of like introducing myself to him. The real me. To give him when I find him.

If he wants to know me. And look at my drawings. And read my notebook. To find out who I am. His daughter.

I write letters to him, in my notebook. About how much I want to know him.

Mom calls these times when you can't sleep night worries. She says everything gets brighter when daylight comes to chase worries away. But next morning, when sunlight is pouring into the kitchen and hurting my head and I'm pouring cereal for Daisy and making cheese toast with raspberry jam for me, I just want to crawl back to my bed and hide under the duvet.

Like, forever.

And hope those worries aren't already there, waiting to grab me.

What I really don't want to do is go to school. And maybe see Julia. Or Candy and Tiffany, her two bully-helpers. I heard that Julia's still here in Seabright. Some kids said that her dad wants her to go to this really expensive private school, but she didn't get in yet. Until she does, she's probably still going to be at Evangeline, just like me and Jayden and Sam. And our other friends.

twelve

Unless she got suspended. Is what she did bad enough for that? I know the police said she has to do community service and go to counselling, but I don't think there was anything about her having to stay away from me or being suspended from school.

Or can you even get suspended, if your father is the principal? I have no idea. Adults don't tell kids anything about stuff like this.

thirteen

I feel so awful I want to stay home from school.

Mom puts her hand on my forehead and says, "No, that's not going to happen, Morley. You don't have a fever, or a cold. And I'm pretty sure you don't have flu. You'll feel much better once your day gets started." So I have to go.

I watch out for Julia all day. If she's there, I don't see her. That's a relief. For one day, at least.

After school, I leave a note for Mum saying I'm going for a bike ride and head over to Mr. Ferguson's house.

I knock on the door of the workshop. Then I wait. And knock again.

"Oh, it's you," he says when he answers. "What do you want?"

"I want to come in. Just to visit. For a minute." I say.

"Oh, ho, a visitor, eh? Checking up on old Gus, are

thirteen

you? Or just here to be nosy?"

"Just here to talk to you...and...uh, find out what you do. Here. In your, um, garage?"

"Workshop," he says, stepping aside. "It's my workshop. I make boxes. Fancy boxes. Like for jewellery cases or just to keep things in. Blanket boxes. Some folks use 'em for end tables."

"Is that your business?" I ask, fingering one of the sleek boxes on his workbench. "Can I open it?"

"Hobby, more like. Sure, go ahead."

The box is made of beautiful coloured woods, very smooth and shiny. The top has a fossil of a sea shell set in it. I think it's beautiful and tell Mr. Ferguson that. Inside the box there's a little shelf that fits right in, with spaces where you could keep earrings, or rings, or other small things that are special.

"Yeah, well..." he says.

Girl...Feather says, just waking up. He stretches and walks over to rub against my leg.

Morley, I say to him. *You remember me, don't you?* I reach down to pet him.

"Well, ain't that something?" Mr. Ferguson says. "That cat won't have nothing to do with me. But he walks right over to cozy up to you. Like you're best pals!"

I smile and lift Feather onto my lap, running my hands down his sides. He's thinner than he was last time I did this. I can easily feel his ribs. And his coat isn't shiny, like it should be.

Don't worry, I tell him. *I have food for you and a plan for how you're going to be OK.*

When Mr. Ferguson doesn't notice, I slip a little plastic container of cat food out of my pocket, peel the lid back and put it on the floor, over in the corner behind the wood pile. Feather runs over and starts eating.

Mr. Ferguson shows me some more about how he makes his boxes.

I tell him about how I make my bracelets and sell them at the Saturday Market. He says that might be an idea for his boxes. Though he spends so long making each box, it would be hard to part with it. Unless it was to someone who would really treasure it.

Like I treasure Feather, I think.

"Because they aren't just boxes. They're more like art," I say. It just pops out of my mouth before I even think it.

Mr. Ferguson looks surprised. "Yes, young lady. That's it exactly," he says. "Uh, what did you say your name is, again?"

He's smiling now and only looks a little bit grouchy when I leave. He says it's fine if I want to come back tomorrow.

So I do. With Feather's food dish and a bag of cat food and a couple of the toys I bought for him. And some of mom's mint chocolate chip cookies for Gus.

They both seem pretty happy to see me. Mr. Ferguson even has a snack for me. Store-bought oatmeal cookies and a can of cola. They're not my favourites,

thirteen

but I eat them to be polite.

Feather is really happy to get the kitten food. It's chicken flavour, I tell Mr. Ferguson. Just to find out if he likes it. I already know that just about all cats like chicken flavour dry cat food. Unless they're really, really sick. Then they need special wet food.

Mr. Ferguson seems happy to see me. Not nearly as grouchy as he was the first time I came here, with Aunt Eira.

I think maybe he is kind of lonely, since he retired. He told me that he was married once, a long time ago, but he doesn't have any children. Or grandchildren. He doesn't say where his wife went. But I think maybe she left him.

The next time I go over to see him, I take more food for Feather and more cookies and a big slab of Mom's apple carrot cake for Gus. I also take some bracelets I made to show him. And a man bracelet I made for him. He says he never was much of a one for jewellery, but he puts his gift bracelet on anyways.

He's got this huge boot thing on his left leg. It kind of looks like a moon astronaut boot and covers his whole foot and leg, almost up to his knee. He says it's a damn fool thing but he did something to his foot and now he has to wear this blasted thing. He can still kind of walk, but he says it's hard to sit up at his bench and work with that damned thing on his leg.

It reminds me of all the different casts I had on my arm, until I finally didn't have to wear one any more.

I make him a cup of coffee and open mom's cookies

107

and tell him about stuff like riding horses with Jayden and learning how to dive with Sam at her pool and how much fun her Hawaii-theme birthday party was. Just about our whole grade 5 class and the other grade 5, Jayden's class, was there. It really was EPIC, just like Sam promised.

I tell him about starting up the Pet Club at school and my art lessons last summer with Maudie Lewis. And about Daisy's princess book and Mom having a baby pretty soon, but we don't know if it's going to be a boy or a girl. That's because Mom says she doesn't want to know until they're born. She says it's supposed to be a surprise.

Mr. Ferguson tells me to call him Gus. He's easy to talk to. He mostly listens. Sometimes, he asks a question.

And sometimes he tells me about how he was a policeman, when he was a young man. Then he was in the Army. After that, he was a teacher for a while. Then he worked at the Y until he retired.

He says he misses it sometimes, but it's good to have his own home. And his workshop. And his boxes to make.

He's not like that crabby man Aunt Eira and I met, just a few weeks ago.

Some days, Sam or Jayden comes over to Mr. Ferguson's with me. And, a few times at first, Aunt Eira did. Just to make sure, she says, that it's all right.

I've already told her that Gus is OK. He's a friend.

fourteen

How did you know the workshop was on fire?

How did you know the owner was inside?

Why didn't you call 9-1-1 and wait for the emergency responders?

What time did you arrive at Mr. Ferguson's house? Why were you there?

Was anyone else there? Did you see anyone else there, or anyone leaving? Running away...?

It's hard to answer. My throat is so dry and raw, I can't talk. I have to write down the answers, even though my hands hurt so much.

It's like after I woke up in hospital. Except now, it feels like my whole body is full of black smoke. I can feel it, rolling around inside me.

My mouth tastes like I've been eating ashes from a

campfire. It's hard to breathe. And I'm so tired.

But I can't sleep. Because as soon as I close my eyes, I see it all again. Feel it all again. The heat is burning my face and slamming up against my body, like being inside a furnace.

The roaring sound in my ears is like some monster beast. A black bear, maybe. Or a dragon.

There's so much smoke that I can't see anything, can't find Mr. Ferguson, can't find the way out.

Like being trapped inside a horror movie of heat and smoke.

And noise.

My mother and Daisy went to bed long ago. I can still hear my aunt and Dom, talking out in the kitchen. Answering the phone, even though it's the middle of the night. It's journalists and bloggers calling, they say, as well as emailing and texting. Wanting to know more about the story. Not caring that it's so late at night.

My aunt and Dom have written what they call a statement from our family, which is just like a page answering the questions everyone is asking. They put it on Facebook and other places online.

But still, people keep calling. And asking the same things. Over and over.

I know my aunt and Dom are tired too. But they're staying up so my mom and I don't have to. They're drinking coffee, answering emails, responding to texts and monitoring comments on social media.

fourteen

For a while, I stayed up with them, wrapped in blankets, sipping cool water, until my mother made me go to bed. Sleep, she says, is what I need now.

I can't sleep.

She doesn't know that trying to sleep takes me back there. Back to the heat and noise and fear of Mr. Ferguson's workshop. On fire.

The people who call say they want to speak to the young girl who is being hailed as a hero. That's what the TV news said.

Even though I can't talk.

I don't feel like a hero. I just wish they'd all go away. And leave me alone to go find Feather, because he's still out there. He's alone.

I can't hear him.

I can't talk to him. I know he must be even more frightened than I was.

Am.

I picture him, hiding somewhere, not understanding what happened. Not knowing the dangers now, but being scared. And alone. And hungry.

Because, like poor Gus, his home is gone.

The happy news is that Mr. Ferguson is safe. He's at the hospital tonight, being cared for. Not hurt seriously, the doctor said. He should be ready to go home just as soon as they're sure his breathing is good.

But where will that be? His home is destroyed.

The only good thing about the fire is that no one was seriously hurt.

The doctor said they'll keep Gus - Mr. Ferguson – in hospital "for observation." That means to watch and be careful, because he is an older person. He's 77, he told me. And healthy, but it might take him longer to feel better than it takes me. Because I'm a kid. Kids heal faster.

Here's how it started. That was just hours ago, I remind myself, just this afternoon. Or maybe it's so late, that was yesterday. It feels like days ago. Weeks ago. Not like it just happened.

So now, I'm sitting up in bed with my notebook and my flashlight, writing about it. Very slowly, because my hands are bandaged. They got a bit burnt.

But I have to write it all down. Everything I can remember.

Here are the things I know. We learned them in grade 4. When there's an emergency, like a fire, you always dial 911 first.

If you're in a fire, check any surface, like a door, with the back of your hand, and if it's hot, don't open it.

Don't use the palm of your hand, because palms burn much more easily than the skin on the back of your hand.

Never, ever go into a burning building.

Call for help. Wait for help to arrive. Do what the first responders and the firefighters and the police tell you to do.

fourteen

We learned all that at school.

Today, I broke just about every one of these fire safety rules.

When I got to Mr. Ferguson's place, I went in the side door of the house.

It was his birthday, he said, and he and I were going to have a little celebration. Eira, too, and Jayden and Sam, if they wanted to come.

But they were all busy, so it was just me.

I get there and find the door unlocked, just like it usually is. We live in small towns, Gus says. Most folks don't bother locking anything.

I leave my bike outside and let myself into the house, calling out for Gus.

No answer.

Then I smell smoke. There's a store cake on the table and plates set out and the radio is turned on. So Gus must be home. But he isn't in the kitchen, or the dining room, or the living room, or the sunroom at the back. I run upstairs, where it's even more smoky, shouting his name and calling for Feather.

I race through every room looking. They aren't there.

Then I come outside and take some deep breaths of air. I look up and see that now there are flames shooting out the upstairs windows. The workshop is right behind the house, attached to it by a little hallway that Mr. Ferguson calls the breezeway. It's crammed with old furniture and stuff that blocks the inside door to the workshop.

That wouldn't stop the fire! I know it could easily spread from the house to the workshop.

Where Gus and Feather must be.

I run to the outside door to the workshop. For some reason, it's jammed.

"Mr. Ferguson," I scream. "GUS, are you in there? Your house is on fire!"

No answer.

I pound my whole body against the door, but it wouldn't budge.

Then there's a *BOOM!*

The entire house is one big fire! But why aren't there any sirens coming? Surely someone with a phone has seen the smoke coming from Mr. Ferguson's house?

They must be coming. I just can't hear them.

Until they get here, I'm the only one who can save them.

fifteen

I still have my packsack. I pull out my gym shirt, empty my water bottle on it and wrap the wet shirt around my neck.

Then I look all around the door and find a small piece of wood, wedged in from the outside. Like what Gus calls a shim. It's what's wedging the door closed. So it would be impossible for anyone inside to get out. I know there are windows, but they don't open.

Someone must have put the skim in the door. From the outside. I can't stop now to think about why. Or who.

I pull at this shim and dug around it. It seems like a long time, but I get it out and throw it away.

A wall of smoke comes tumbling out as I yank the door open, shouting for Mr. Ferguson.

A black streak races past me.

Feather.

Feather, I call to him. *Where is he? The man? Where?*

Fire, fire, fire, run. RUN, he says.

Mr. Ferguson, I say to Feather. *WHERE IS HE?*

Run. Run. Hide. Run.

I wrap the wet shirt around my face and plunge into the smoky room.

I've been in the workshop so often, I know where everything is. I feel my way around, searching for Gus, because the smoke is now so thick my eyes are streaming with tears. I almost can't see. Or breathe.

I find the wood box.

I stumble over Mr. Ferguson's easy chair.

And stub my toes on the rocking chair, where I sometimes sit with Feather on my lap.

I stumble around in the smoky dark, looking for Gus. Mr. Ferguson. My friend.

Feeling to find out where I am. Trying to move quickly. And bumping into things. Because even when you think you know a room, when it's on fire, somehow, everything is different.

Nothing is where you expect it to be.

It's so easy to get confused.

I hear myself coughing and hacking away. I can't get enough air!

fifteen

It feels like my lungs are going to explode.

Everything in me wants to turn back for the door. Or where I think the door must be.

Soon, I'm totally turned around. It's like stumbling around in a black cave where you are almost blind, your eyes are watering so much.

Where your ears work, but the fire is so loud, the fire is all you can hear.

The fire claws at me, grabbing at my clothes, stealing all the air.

"Gus," I try to call, as loud as I can. But it comes out like a choked sound. Not nearly loud enough.

Very soon, I know I have to turn back to find the door or I'll be trapped by this fire. Devoured by it.

Gus isn't near his workbench. Or sleeping in his easy chair. Or up in the loft, where he keeps his apple wood drying. Finally, I find him, on the floor, next to the breezeway door.

He's trying to pull off the moon boot. But it's stuck.

"GUS!" I scream, as loud as I can as close to his good ear as I can get. "We have to get out of here. NOW. Come on!"

I take the wet shirt away from my face that was helping me breath and wrap it around his face.

I get down close to the floor and rip at the bands that keep the moon boot closed. Finally, I can pull it off his leg.

I try to haul Gus up to his feet.

I put his hand on my shoulder and tug him towards the door.

Where I hope the door is.

He keeps trying to pull us back. I think he must be confused about where he is.

I kept hacking and gasping for breath.

And using all my strength, everything I've got left to pull him behind me.

I need air.

I'm so tired, I just want to lie down on the floor and sleep.

My hands and my face are burning.

Then I think I see just a glimmer of light. Like a tiny little star. Far away.

Just a speck, like one star peeking through the clouds on a stormy night.

It's the door to outside. It has to be!

"Have to go back," Mr. Ferguson gasps, trying to pull me back with him.

"NO!" I scream, as loud as I can. With my very last bit of strength, I grab him and pull him towards the speck of light.

sixteen

It gets bigger.

I gasp for air and try again to move us both closer to that light. Hoping, wishing, praying that it's the door.

Gasping for air.

Tugging on Gus. Hoping he has enough strength to make it to the door.

That we both do.

Then we tumble forward.

We both fall on the ground, gasping for air.

And then there is shouting and hands are grabbing us and somebody is putting a mask with lovely fresh air over my face.

Then I'm sitting in an ambulance, wrapped in a silver foil blanket and sweating and shivering at the same time.

"Where is Gus?" I try to say, but it just sounds like a

croak.

"No talking, now," a woman in a blue uniform says. "Keep that mask on, it will help." Then I hear more sirens and know it's more help on the way. Mr. Ferguson must have a blanket and an air mask like I do.

Then my mother is there, shrieking and crying and trying to hug me and having the ambulance people pull her away.

I have to go to hospital. But after a few hours of being looked at and getting a chest x-ray and cream and bandages on my hands and face and legs, they say I can go home.

Just so long as I come back the next day to check my hands, the skin on my face that's starting to feel like it's stretched too tight and my feet. They got a bit burnt, too.

Aunt Eira and Dom say they'll stay up and watch me, because Mom being so pregnant means she has to get some sleep. Especially after a big shock like this.

I lay in bed, feeling that sticky stuff they put on my face and hands and feet, trying not to sleep and have another one of those nightmares about still being in the fire.

I touch my left wrist and realize my new Wish Bracelet isn't there.

I turn on my bedtime reading flashlight to check.

The gold bead wish bracelet is gone. The one with the wish to have Gus decide that I can have Feather.

sixteen

It must have happened when I was trying to get the door open. Or inside the workshop, when I was trying to tug Mr. Ferguson out of his workshop. I didn't even notice. I guess those wish beads must have got burnt up in the fire.

Like all Mr. Ferguson's beautiful boxes. All his tools, and his applewood and cherry wood. His workbench, and everything else in his workshop. And everything in his house. And his car, too. I remember it was parked in the driveway, right next to the house.

Poor Gus. He's lost every single thing he owns, except the clothes he had on. At the hospital, they gave him a blue gown to put on. Mom said she'd take his clothes home and launder them for him.

They have burn holes and they smell so much of smoke, I wonder if Mom will be able to get the smoke smell out of them. Or if he'll ever want to wear them again.

Wouldn't they remind him of that terrible time, when we couldn't find our way out of his burning workshop?

That's how I felt about my clothes. Even though it was my favourite yellow sweater I had on, and my almost-new red puffer coat, and my favourite pair of jeans.

I asked Eira to put them all in the garbage.

Mom said she understood.

Right after we got home from hospital, two police officers came to talk to me. Again, as my mother says. Wanting to know why I was there.

At Gus' house.

If I was the one who started the fire.

If so, why I'd do a terrible thing like that.

Because they say they know the fire didn't start by accident.

It wasn't because Mr. Ferguson wasn't careful with tools or with the wood stove. I already knew that. He'd shown me how to sand wood properly and how to care for tools and how to build a fire in the wood stove.

I know he's too smart and too careful to accidentally set his home and his workshop on fire.

Someone started that fire.

That's what I told the police officer.

No, I didn't know why.

I didn't know who.

I didn't see anyone else there.

So how did I know that someone wanted to hurt Gus? Why would I say that?

Because of the shim. Under the door. I explained about it to the police.

It took them a while to understand what I was telling them.

They said possibly I was wrong? Because who'd want to hurt a kindly old man like Mr. Ferguson?

I can't answer this question. I tell them what I know. About looking everywhere in his house. About the wood shim under the door and how hard I had to

sixteen

scrape to get it out.

About searching everywhere for him.

About pulling him outside.

Their faces turned from looking like they didn't believe me to looking shocked.

My mother looked angry.

"Attempted murder..." she said.

"Now, we don't know that yet," the woman police officer said. "But we are investigating this fire. It does appear that it could be suspicious at this time."

My throat hurts so much that I have to write answers to the police questions. It's hard and slow, because my hands are hurting inside the bandages. It doesn't feel like burning. More like the worst sunburn you could possibly have. Like your skin is just about burnt off.

They say I was lucky to get out alive, with so few injuries. And so was Mr. Ferguson.

And that, whoever it was who set the fire, if someone did which is possible, they'll find them. But they need to find more witnesses.

And if there is what they call "sufficient evidence" they will prosecute them. "Don't worry, Ms. Star. We'll find out what happened!" they say as they're leaving. "Get well, Morley!"

When they've gone, my mother goes to bed. Eira goes to the all-night convenience store and buys me popsicles. And ice cream. Cool for your throat, she says.

She sits with me for a while. Not saying anything. It's good to have her there. Then she says she had to go back and help Dom. But she'll keep checking on me. And my mom. Who'd been so frightened...

Probably not half as much as I was.

seventeen

Here's the story from the newspaper:

Seabright Girl Rescues Local Senior

An 11-year-old Seabright girl, Morley Star, is being hailed as a hero after rescuing Noble 'Gus' Ferguson, 77, from a housefire in Port Loring Wednesday that police are now calling "suspicious."

"We've had a number of small fires in and around Seabright in the past several weeks that may be related," police spokesperson Constable Teresa Wright said. "This includes trash bin fires behind restaurants and next to apartment blocks and at homes of summer residents normally empty at this time of year. We're asking the public for any information they may have about these fires."

She added that the fire that drew responders from the Fire Departments of Seabright, Minas Bay, Loring and Port Williams to Mr. Ferguson's home and workshop is considered to be "suspicious and possibly deliberate," pending investigation by the County Fire Marshall's office.

Constable Wright would not say anything further about the cause of the fire in a residential area of the village near Seabright. But, she added, the home and property are "extensively fire damaged."

The two occupants of the property at the time of the incident both escaped with "minor injuries," police say.

The home was totally engulfed in flames when fire departments arrived. Owner of the home, Noble Ferguson, remains in hospital under observation, while Miss Star was treated and released for burns to her legs, hands and face.

Mr. Ferguson was not available for comment, but Miss Star's family have released a statement saying that she was visiting Mr. Ferguson for a birthday celebration when she saw smoke. Not finding him in the house, she went looking for him in his workshop, which was also on fire.

"We are very grateful for the fast response of the first responders," the Star family statement said. "And also very grateful that both Morley and Gus Ferguson have survived."

The family also thanked the many friends and

seventeen

neighbours who have already reached out with offers to help Mr. Ferguson, whose home police and firefighters declared uninhabitable following the fire, which was finally brought under control five hours after first responders arrived.

Police are appealing for information about this incident and other recent fires in the area.

The next day, my face and hands hurt so much that when Dr. Carolyn changed the bandages, she gave me some painkillers. She said I probably should rest as much as possible for a few days, at least.

All I wanted to do was sleep. With no nightmares.

And when I woke up, go find Feather.

Because it wasn't very lucky for him that, once again, he'd lost his home.

Just like Mr. Ferguson had.

Which made me think about how would Gus be able to come home from hospital? What home would he go to, now that his home and everything he had was gone? His furniture. His car. Even his clothes.

Mom says perhaps he has friends to stay with, until he finds another place to live.

"But what if he'd like to live here?" I ask, thinking out loud. "He could have the garden bedroom. And eat with us. That way, he wouldn't have to go find a new place to live and buy everything again, like a chair and a bed and sheets and towels...and everything. At least not right away."

My mom smiles. "That could be one of your best ideas yet, Morley!" she says. "I wonder if he'd like that? I'll ask him today when I'm there." It was one of her days to get a scan of the baby. That's a test they do to check that a baby is OK, before it's born. Afterwards, she said, she'd just see if she could find Gus' room. And take him some cookies. And see that he's comfortable.

Since kids aren't allowed to visit and sitting in the waiting room wasn't what Daisy or I wanted to do while Mom went to see Gus, Mom dropped us off at Aunt Eira's.

"I've been thinking about something," I say, munching on the tuna melt sandwiches we make for lunch. "Gus hasn't got anything any more…"

"Yes, that's true. Poor man," my aunt says.

"So how can he leave the hospital?"

"What do you mean?" She cuts the crusts off Daisy's sandwich and opens her tangerine for her, separating the slices.

"You know how the fire made my jeans and jacket a mess, with burn marks and they all are so smoky I don't ever want to wear them again? Mum said we could just wash them, but…they remind me of…"

Eira puts her hand on my shoulder. "I know what you mean. That's why you asked me to throw them away."

"Do you think what Gus had on got ruined, too? How can he get out of hospital if he doesn't have anything to wear?"

"Like no coat. And no shoes." Daisy says. "Because they got all wrecked in the fire..."

"So he doesn't even have anything at all now."

"Of course. We should have thought of that already. What do you want to do about it?"

Dom has been doing something on his laptop and munching on his own sandwich, but now he looks up. "We could ask around, I mean for donations of clothing. And I might have a couple of things that would fit him..."

I think Gus would hate that, if we were asking people to give him their clothes. "Why don't we buy him some new things? You know, it was his birthday, and he never did get to open his presents..." I think of the painting I did for him as his gift. Burnt up, like everything else.

At least I can make that picture again and give it to him. We could have another birthday party for Gus. When he's feeling better.

"What sort of clothes?" Daisy says.

"Well, socks and underwear for a start," Eira says.

"I can handle getting that, easy enough" Dom says. "I meant to get some new undies for myself. Just as easy to buy extras."

"But do we know his size?" Eira says. "And what sort of clothes does he like? I don't remember if he wears jeans, or did he have on an overall? Morley, do you remember?"

"He likes old, sort of worn out clothes that are kind of

baggy," I say, picturing him in his workshop...before. The way it was when I used to visit him there. "And he's about as tall as Dom, but wider in the middle."

"Size XL should do," Dom says. "You're just getting him enough to wear until he can go out and get what he wants, right? So why don't I take Daisy and we'll get him some socks and underwear, and maybe look for a pair of shoes while you two get him some jeans and shirts. And a jacket."

"Where would be good, do you think? Would Phinney's have anything?" Eira asks.

"Naw, that's just tourist stuff like tee shirts. You could drive up to the city?"

But I have a better idea. "Daisy and I got our Halloween outfits at Value Village," I say, "and Mom is always saying how she found a great sweater or a handbag or something there that was almost new. We could look there."

So that's where we go. It doesn't take long to find some soft gray jogging pants, three plain tee shirts, a gray sweater and a navy jacket. We also find some men's gloves and a man's green bathrobe that is as soft as old towels. I'm amazed when all of it costs about the same as just buying a plain jacket at the mall. "It can be my gift," Eira says, pulling out her charge card.

"If everything's a bit too big, that's probably OK," I say. "I think Gus picks out clothes to be comfortable. I don't think he really cares how they look. But these all look like what he likes." Best of all, they don't smell of smoke. They wouldn't remind him of the fire.

seventeen

We get back to Aunt Eira's at just about the same time as Dom and Daisy. They cut the tags off everything, launder it, fold it all and put it in one of Dom's spare sports bags.

Eira says she'll take his new wardrobe to Gus after she drops us off at home.

Two days later, Gus comes home to our house. I thought it was wonderful that he'd have his own space upstairs, but it would be like he was part of our family.

Mom invites him to be a long-term paying guest until his house is built again and ready to live in. That will probably be by next summer. Or maybe he'll want to live in an apartment. Or buy a different house. He says he's not ready to decide about that.

I feel so sorry for him, losing everything he owned. But I think maybe it makes him feel a bit better to be with me and Daisy and Mom. And sometimes Eira and Dom. He's not alone.

He says he knows his home is gone. He doesn't want to go back and see how bad things are. Not yet. He thanks Eira for everything, including offering to drive him to his old house, or where it used to be. But no, he says. He isn't ready to face it.

He's talked to the police. And his lawyer. And made a list of everything that was in his house and workshop for the insurance company.

"You'll be needing another car," Dom says. "I'll be happy to drive you around to look, when you're ready."

Gus wants to know about how others on his street are

doing, especially the closest neighbours. Was there smoke or fire damage next door, at the Maclean's house and over on the other side, the Yaski family? If so, he hopes it wasn't too bad. He asks if maybe Eira could find out.

I didn't want to go back to school. Not yet. My hands were still hurting and wrapped in bandages. But they were healing properly, the doctor said. And I still limp a little bit, because the fire hurt the bottom of my feet. But they're getting better.

I'd been begging Eira to take me back to Mr. Ferguson's, just about since it happened. She knows it wasn't because I want to see the destroyed house. I have to find Feather.

She went over there and put out a bowl of water and a bowl of cat food. She did that every day, but she never saw him.

She didn't think there was much chance that I could find him, if she couldn't.

So that's when I told her the secret I've kept for so long. That I can hear Feather in my mind. If he was there, and if he was awake, and if he could, he'd let me know.

eighteen

She didn't laugh.

She didn't say you must be crazy.

She didn't say it's all in your imagination.

She just said, "Come on. Get in the car. I'll tell your mom we're just getting you out of the house. That you need some fresh air!"

It was a beautiful fall day. Cool, but the sky was that intense autumn blue. The leaves were gold and orange and red on some trees, though lots of leaves were on the ground now.

The trees in Mr. Ferguson's yard were all bare. The trunks were scorched black. I wondered if they would come back to life in the spring. Or if the fire has killed them.

I guess we'll have to wait and see.

The house and workshop are just a black pile of burnt wood, bent metal and broken things. I wrap a scarf around my face, because even a breeze touching my skin makes it hurt.

Eira gets out of the car, comes around and undoes my seat belt, because my hands can't do that yet. She helps me out of the car.

We walk around, not very close to the place Mr. Ferguson's house used to be, because there is still yellow police tape stretched all around it. They said on the news it was a crime scene. That is because police are now saying someone started that fire.

They meant to do harm.

Maybe to hurt Mr. Ferguson. Or maybe just to see his home burn down so he'd have to move.

Today, the street is quiet. There's no one around. People who live here must all be at work. Or at school.

"Here, kitty, kitty, kitty," Eira says.

Feather, I call, in my head. *It's me. Morley. Come out, Feather. Please.*

Nothing.

I'm here to help you. I want to help you.

Nothing.

You can't live outside. You're an indoor cat. You aren't meant to live like a wild cat.

Still nothing.

Feather, I need you to come out because...because I need you. I need to hold you. I need to see you, every day. I need you in my life.

Hiding, he says in a thin little voice. *Scared.*

Home, I say. *Come home where it's warm and safe. There are good things to eat there. I'm there to take care of you.*

Afraid, he says. *Hiding.*

"You're talking to him, aren't you?" Eira says.

I nod.

"Where is he?"

"Nearby. I'm not sure where exactly."

The fire is gone. All gone. The strangers are gone. There is just me here. Me and my aunt. But you are in danger here.

Silence.

Cars could hit you. There might be dogs out, or other cats that want to fight. And it's getting colder out. Winter is coming. It will be even harder for you to live outside. You can't kill your own food. I know you didn't learn how. So you will be very hungry. Wouldn't you rather have a full food dish and be in a warm house, with me?

Then, crawling out from under the front porch of the house across the street, I see a little black and white head. Followed by a mostly black body with white paws.

"Oh," Eira says, standing next to me as Feather walks over and brushes up against my legs. I reach down to pick him up. It hurts, but I do it anyways.

I sink my face into his fur, smelling the sweet scent of

him. Today, he smells like fresh laundry and Christmas trees.

And then he starts to purr. *Home*, he says. *Home.*

Home is when I'm with you, I tell him.

"Home," Eira says as she puts Feather in the pet carrier box we brought. She puts it on the back seat, turning it so Feather can see me. Then she does up my seat belt. "Let's go."

And then it's coming up to Thanksgiving. My hands and face and feet get better. I go back to school.

Life goes on.

Pretty much the way it was before, except better because now, Feather sleeps curled up beside me. His food dish and water dish are in the kitchen, next to the fridge. And he sits in the front window sometimes, watching birds.

We're safe. We're together.

And we're home.

nineteen

Aunt Eira and Sam made the bracelets, in the weeks that I couldn't. And she took over the Saturday Market with Mom's two helpers, now that mom is so pregnant that, she says, "Everything is a huge effort!"

I was just grateful Mom invited Gus to come and live with us. He was getting better, like I was. Sometimes, he'd read to Daisy, or play Candyland with her, or Crazy 8s.

Or play old-fashioned tunes on the piano in the living room. I didn't know he could do that!

He taught me how to play chess and told Mum not to worry, he'd look after the fall yard-work and getting the tools put away for winter.

There wasn't a lot I could do until my hands healed. I went to physio to learn some exercises to get them working right again. Those exercises hurt, but I needed to get my hands stronger to be able to make jewellery and art.

Sam and Jayden came over every day. They always had news and stories from school. They made me feel like I wasn't missing out on everything.

They said that Julia did some other mean stuff and the stories came out about other kids she hurt. Then she got mad at a teacher and stabbed the teacher in the hand with a pencil. That got Julia suspended. So now there's an investigation into bullying at our school. They said the police came to talk to all the students about how serious violence is and that it's a crime.

While they were there, the police asked if anybody knew anything about who might be starting the fires. Nobody said anything. They said kids could call the kids' help line, if they're bullied and need to talk to someone. And they could call Crime Stoppers if they know anything about the fires.

Liam, a boy in my class that I like, is now the leader of the Pet Club.

Mr. Cadeau came to our house three times a week to be sure I wouldn't fall behind in grade six. Mom said I should be grateful because he came on his own time, and what a special thing it is that he'd do this to help us. He said it was nothing, compared to what I did and how proud everyone who knows me is. That makes me smile.

No one was prouder, or more grateful, than Mr. Ferguson. He is always thanking me for saving his life, because he's sure he wouldn't have gotten out of that fire if I didn't come over that day. And make him

nineteen

leave the burning workshop.

He says he's so sorry that I came over to visit and ended up getting hurt.

And he's thanking my mother and our family for giving him a new home. One that already has a comfortable bed and a reading chair right next to the window in his room and a place to make his tea and, he says, everything he needs.

He started making his beautiful boxes again out in our garage, where Mom and I used to fix up her yard sale and used store finds. All that stuff we bought at yard sales is stacked up at one end, since she says in her condition, she means about having the baby, she won't be refinishing furniture any time soon.

And Feather has settled into our family. But mostly, into my life. "He's your cat, no question about it," Mr. Ferguson says at supper one day. Gus has most of his meals with us now. Mum says she couldn't imagine a more gracious guest. I know that pleases Mr. Ferguson.

It's surprising how he just fits in with our family. Like he's always been here.

It was Jayden who had the really brilliant idea about him having a cat, when he gets his new house built. Mr. Ferguson says he thought it might be some time before he has his own place again because he's so comfortable living with us, but when he does, he might just want a good mouser. Not Feather, he says, who never did take much to being a working cat.

When I tell him why, that cats know how to hunt but

they need their mother to teach them how to kill their prey and Feather's mother never taught him that, Gus is amazed. "Never quite thought of it that way," he says.

Jayden had the idea that what Mr. Ferguson really needs isn't a PET cat, like Feather, but a professional BARN cat. Maybe one of the ones from his family's barns. Or there is the barn cat adoption program at the pet shelter.

Mr. Ferguson had no idea there was a difference between types of cats, depending on the job they do. I remembered about feral cats and barn cats being sort of like pet cats, but not really, from what Jayden said when we worked on my Get-A-Pet project.

Mr. Ferguson says he's very interested to learn that.

Feather likes to curl up in my closet, on my pile of sweaters, and sleep.

Or try to paw at the bugs that get trapped between the window and the screen.

Or hop up on my desk and knock things on the floor.

Or suddenly decide to race up and down the stairs for no reason except one only cats know. He won't tell me why.

Aunt Eira took pictures of me with Feather and wrote on her blog about how important it is to help pets who need homes. She told about how, by asking for donations and making bracelets and doing pet portraits, I had been able to donate more than $2,500 to the Sunflower Pet Shelter.

nineteen

She wrote that it just shows what a kid can do. That you don't need to be an adult to be creative, show compassion to others in need and make a difference.

Someone from the newspaper must have read that blog post, because then there are lots of reporters calling who want to talk to me about it. And get some pictures of me with Gus and Feather.

And then the directors of Sunflower Pet Shelter want to meet me. Mom thinks it might be so they can shake my hand and thank me for being a volunteer and giving them the donation money. She wonders why they didn't do this already.

She's right. They say, "Thank you Morley for being our first junior volunteer and raising money for the pets." And they all want to shake my hand. That was good, except for this one man that squeezed my hand too hard and it hurt.

But even better was when Mrs. Piers-Smythe had a question. She's a lady that looks a little bit like grandad's wife, Margie. Mrs. Piers-Smythe is the Chairman of the Board of Directors – they're the bosses – at Sunflower Pet Shelter. She said she and all the other board members wondered if maybe I know kids like me who might want to be junior volunteers at the shelter? Maybe I could ask my friends at school?

I said I'd see. But what I really want to tell them about is some ideas I've got that kids would like that would raise more money to save more pets.

"Extraordinary!" Mrs. Piers-Smythe says. "And what might these ideas be?"

"I'd rather make a presentation," I tell her. I could already picture it in my head. The slides I'd make, the drawings I'd do, the research I need to do. It was just like my Get-A-Pet project. Only bigger.

"And you can't just tell us now?"

"It would be better if I could give you all the information. I need to get ready to do that," I say.

I see the other adults around the table nodding in agreement. Next to me, my mom smiles. Good. It feels exciting to have another project to do.

Mrs. Piers-Smythe and all the directors agree that I am invited to their next general meeting, in December, to present my ideas for involving kids and young volunteers in helping the pet shelter.

"Good for you," my mother says after that, when we're driving home. "You stood right up and said your piece, just like a grown-up. Are you pleased that they said they'd listen to your ideas?"

I was grinning so much, I thought she'd already know how pleased I am. And proud.

And happy.

twenty

Gus and Dom must have gone to every used car place there is, here and then up in the city.

Sometimes, Daisy and I went with them. It was fun. Usually, Dom drove and sometimes, Gus pulled out his harmonica and we all sang funny songs.

Gus looked at trucks. He did test drives in regular cars and even thought about maybe having a van. For a while, he had this crazy idea about buying an old delivery truck and turning it into a camper van. What he finally bought is a SUV.

He chose it, he said, because it was easy to get into and out of. And he liked how high up you sit in an SUV, so you can see everything. And there's plenty of space in the back. But it's still easy to park.

He said he's happy to get a good reliable car and have his freedom again. And would I like to go search for some fossils?

And did Daisy want to come, too?

Daisy said sure, if we could go to Mickey Dee's first?

So we did. There are a few places around here to find fossils. Down at Blue Beach is one of them. That's where the ocean cuts away at the cliffs right above the shore, eroding it during storms. When this happens, you can find fossils of plants and animals. And, sometimes, little pieces of things that people used long ago, like arrow heads.

But today, we aren't going to Blue Beach. Instead, we're going to an old quarry, up on English Mountain Road. It belongs to one of Gus' friends, so we have permission to look there for fossils.

Gus shows us how to spot the kinds of rocks that might have fossils hidden inside.

Then you need to knock them, hard, in just the right spot, to split the rock open.

Usually, there isn't anything inside.

But sometimes, there are tiny shells of sea creatures.

And, if you're really lucky, there's the outline of an ancient fish. Or fern plant. Or insect.

Daisy runs around, stacking up what she calls lucky rocks. She means, ones that might have fossils in them.

I try to knock them open, but my hands are still sore.

We find some interesting things, and a few that Gus says will be really good. There's also one that's so

twenty

special, he says he has to show it to his friend who's a professor at the university. It could be a new discovery, he says.

It just looks like an ordinary fish to me. But, Gus says, it could be 100,000 years old. Maybe even older!

If it is, he says, he'll donate it to the university's collection, so lots of people can get to see it.

……

Gus doesn't ever talk about his home and losing it.

Mom says it's a private thing. And Daisy is not to ask about it.

Aunt Eira says it must hurt too much to talk about. But that he has people around him who care about him, especially me. She says she thinks, if he ever wants to talk about the fire, she's sure he already knows we'll listen.

Meanwhile, it's enough just to keep him company, when he wants it. To find fossils, or out in his new workshop in our garage, where he's got it set up to make his boxes again.

"Can't change the past," he says. "Only thing you can change is right now."

Dom and Eira are over at our place one day in October. Eira is helping Mum get the new baby's room ready. Or corner of mum's room where our new brother, or maybe new sister, will have their crib. For now, Mum says. They'll need a proper bedroom eventually. There isn't possibly enough space for them to be in Daisy's and my room.

"Maybe the new baby can share with Daisy," I say, "And I can have my own room again."

"Well, we'll see," Mom says.

Dom and I are cleaning all the windows. On the inside and also on the outside, as much as you can reach without climbing up a ladder outside. He says he'll do that later.

At the same time, we're taking off the summer screens and stacking them in the basement, ready to go back on the windows next spring.

I like Dom. I wouldn't mind having him for an older brother, if I did have a brother. While we work, he tells me stuff about drawing and designing using a computer. He thinks it's something I might want to try.

And he talks about some places he's been to, like when he worked picking olives in Greece and how interesting it is to explore the markets in Istanbul, and asks if I ever want to travel? Of course I do, I say. As soon as I'm a grown up and I can.

He asks where I want to go first? I say there are so many places, I can't make up my mind. Maybe England, because I want to go on that big ferris wheel they have, only you're inside a little bubble and you can see the whole city.

Dom says that's called the London Eye.

twenty

Or Australia, I say, to see kangaroos.

Or Japan, to ride on a bullet train. Or Paris. Sam liked it there. Or out West, like Jayden did last summer.

He laughs and keeps wiping the window he's doing the high part of, while I wipe the lower part.

I might go to look for my father in Ireland, I think. I know it's not a large country. How hard can it be to find someone there, when you already know their first name?

It's Malcolm. That seems like a funny name. How many men named Malcolm can there be, in Ireland?

I've looked for him on the Internet already, with Eira helping. I think she probably knows where he is, or knows more about him, like his last name. But my mom says I don't need to know that until I'm older. So Eira isn't saying anything else about him.

Yet.

And then it's Thanksgiving.

Mom has decided that making the turkey and a ham and all the trimmings is what she calls, "just too much of too much." So instead, she's booked a table for us at Blomidon Inn. That's an old ship captain's home. He must have had a lot of money and a big family, because it's more like a mansion. Now, it's a place for special occasion meals or having weddings in summer.

The Blomidon Inn people are one of mom's customers for her scones and cakes, so she says she's traded them for our Thanksgiving dinners. She says, for once, Thanksgiving will be a restful day for all of us.

There's seven of us for our special Thanksgiving dinner. Mom, Daisy, me and Mr. Ferguson, except now we call him Uncle Gus. Aunt Eira and Dom. And Danny has come back for a visit. I think of how long I wanted him to be part of our family and I realize now that he is. Just not in the way I thought of, because he doesn't live with us.

I wanted him to come back, but I guess that isn't what he wanted. Or what my mom wanted.

It's strange, but Danny seems so much happier, now that he doesn't live with Daisy, me and mom. They both say that they're better off as friends. And I know he'll keep his promise that he'll always be Daisy's father and want to be in her life.

And the new baby's life.

After the blessing, we eat our turkey and stuffing and cranberry jelly. There's three types of pie for dessert. I choose pumpkin pie, with vanilla ice cream. When we're finished eating, Mom clinks her spoon on her glass and says she wants to say a few words.

She talks about it being a challenging year for us all. In some ways a hard year. But also a year of new beginnings and second chances. I wonder if she's thinking of her new baking business. Or starting the bed-and-breakfast business. Or being able to leave the school secretary job I know she didn't like. Or if she's thinking of the new person in our family who's coming soon.

She talks about happiness, familiar and new.

She talks about giving thanks.

twenty

I think of all I'm thankful for. My family, of course, even though it's different than I thought it would be. I look around the table and realize how much I care about these people.

My new uncle, Gus.

My favourite aunt, Eira.

Even my annoying little sister.

They're my family. The family I wished for and my wish came true.

Both my wishes, because Feather is part of my family now.

Our family.

And I'm thankful for the ones that aren't here right now. Aunt Sorcha and Uncle Chris and their little boys, our cousins.

My best friends Sam and Jayden. Other friends at school and in the pet club.

Mr. Cadeau, who really cares about his students.

My friends at the pet shelter. And at Saturday Market.

Then my mother asks us each to say something we're so thankful for today. Or more than one thing, if we want.

"Well, I'm very thankful I chose the lemon pie, not the pumpkin, though they were both good," Dom says with a grin, after eating all his piece and most of Eira's. "Don't know if I'll feel that way tomorrow, though. Might have to run around Long Lake a few extra times this week to work it off!" He's so skinny that this is ridiculous.

"Oh, you," Eira says, but like all of us, she's laughing.

"Oh yeah, and one other thing I'm grateful for," Dom says. "The most beautiful girl in the world has said she'll marry me. Her name is Ms. Eira Star!"

"YES!" Daisy says, so loud that everyone in the dining room stares at us. "We're having a wedding next year and I'm going to be a bridesmaid!"

"We'll see..." Mom says, leaning over to hug her sister. "I'm so happy for you both."

"I'm grateful for my whole life," Eira says. "Everything and everyone in it! How about you, Gus?"

Mr. Ferguson looks thoughtful. "Well, you all know how I might answer. But right now, I'm thankful to be enjoying this delicious meal with four lovely ladies and, uh, two charming young men."

Daisy says she's grateful that her green Froggie slippers got too small, because she didn't really like them any more and wants new ones for Christmas. Mermaid ones, she says. That's her new thing, that she looks like a girl, but really, she's a mermaid.

Danny says he's grateful for his new job. And he's happy living in the city. But also how good it is to be able to be here in Seabright, where his darling daughter lives and his dear friends the Star family. He says he'll be back at least once a month. And maybe sometimes the Stars will want to come to the city to visit?

"Maybe we will," Mum says. "We'll have to see." She

twenty

says she's thankful for a healthy pregnancy, and that the morning sickness finally went away. And that the next time we're all together, we'll have our new little Star with us.

She means Daisy's and my baby brother. Or sister. Danny reaches over and squeezes her hand. He says he'll be here, when they're born.

Uncle Gus says he forgot to say another thing he's thankful for. That's me and Daisy. "They're the grandchildren I forgot to have," he says, waggling his bushy eyebrows at Daisy to make her giggle. He winks at me.

My hand passes over my wrist as I think of my wishes for this year. My two big wishes. And how they've both come true. Just not quite the way I thought they would.

I have my family, all around me.

And I have Lucky Feather.

So those wish bracelets worked. Both my wishes came true.

It's so pretty when we get home. Just starting to snow. I look in the windows for Feather, but don't see him watching out for us. He must be curled up somewhere, asleep.

"Come on. We have to make snow mermaids!" Daisy says, rushing to get out of the car. Even though it's that time of late afternoon that isn't still the afternoon but isn't evening yet. The blue hour, Ms. Maudie, my art teacher last summer, called it.

The time of magic, she said, for artists.

And, I think, for us all.

Daisy has already thrown herself on the ground to make a snow mermaid.

Why did I look up to the balcony, just then, instead of following everyone but Daisy inside? I can't say. Really, I just don't know.

Except that's what I did. And there was Feather, sitting on the very edge of the railing on the balcony.

"Feather," I shout. "NO!"

But he's jumped up and now…

He's FALLING!

I'm reaching out to him.

Running to catch him.

How could he…but of course. The flies landing on the window screens, and how much he likes to bat at them.

The screens, not on the windows any more, because it's almost winter.

One of those balcony windows left just a little bit open by somebody. Maybe a guest. Or maybe one of us.

Just enough for one small black and white cat to squeeze himself through and get outside. On the balcony.

And up on the railing.

twenty

And fall off.

And I'm running, standing with my arms stretched up.

And he's falling.

And I'm reaching to catch him.

And then he's landed in my arms, cuddled against my coat. And he's purring.

Morley, he says. *My Morley.*

I snuggle him close, keeping him warm, smelling his sweet scent and watching Daisy race around and laugh, trying to catch snowflakes on her tongue.

Snowflakes twinkle as they fall. They sparkle and give me an idea for a bride's crown. You know, the thing she puts in her hair with an up-do. Eira has beautiful long hair, reddish-blonde. I picture the bride's crown I'll make for her. It will be golden, with pearl beads and sparkly crystals like snowflakes. For her spring wedding.

Then mum calls us and we head inside.

Daisy. And me. And Feather.

We're home.

the end

Next In This Series:
Gifted

The whole world, it seems, is getting into the Christmas spirit.

Sam plays Christmas carols at Youth Orchestra concerts and at her school concert. She wraps gifts. She hears about presents under the tree and turkey with stuffing and Christmas with all the trimmings. And all the while, she wonders what it's really like to have a family Christmas?

Stores play Christmas music. Neighbours hang up lights and gather in the town square for the lighting of the giant Christmas tree. At school, kids talk about what presents they hope to get.

But as Sam's mother points out, their heritage is Korean, so they don't "do" Christmas. Or Hanukah. Or Easter. Or Eid. Or any of the other happy holidays that might be celebrated by other people.

The Parks avoid the Holidays, no matter how much Sam wishes this wasn't so. Then something happens that might make the one magical Christmas she's longed for possible!

Read on to find chapter 1 of **Gifted**:

one

I hate airports.

They're cave bubbles connected by hallways. You walk and walk and walk and still it seems you're never getting to where you need to be.

You're always practically running to somewhere, only to stand in another line-up before you can move on. Just hoping you're going to finally get to the right place. At the right time.

After all that rushing, you have to just wait. Sitting in one of those hard plastic chairs. Feeling all jangly and sweaty.

Or you just stand around. Being bored.

There are so many better things you could be doing, if only you weren't stuck here in this stupid airport. You could be hanging out with friends. Riding horses at Jayden's ranch. Making jewellery with Morley. Making enchiladas with Tia Margaret.

Practicing.

Listening to music.

Reading.

Thinking.

Swimming!

But no, you're stuck in some stupid airport.

Where there's all these rules about what you can and can't take with you. Or do. Or say. It's as if, in airports, you're supposed to stop being a person and start being a robot that looks like a person.

One who has to carry too much stuff.

And never needs to pee because you always have to search for the washrooms. When you finally find one, it's probably closed for cleaning. Or there's a line-up.

All of this is bad enough. But it's the sounds of airports that make me want to scream. There's a lot of noise bouncing around and banging into your ears in those hallow buildings.

It's like crackly static in your head, taking up all the space so you can't think.

Or hear the music in your head.

Or just be quiet.

Airports are just about the coldest, unfriendliest, noisiest places I've ever been. Nobody there ever looks happy. Nobody smiles. They all just look like I feel, which is too hot and worried and wishing I could get out of here.

one

There's no point in saying any of this to my mother, who's standing next to me in line, fiddling with her phone. She's a person who's always too cold, even in summer. And she doesn't seem to mind waiting around. She isn't a fan of being inside a plane, even in the front seats where she always sits, but she doesn't mind airports.

"No whining," is what she says to me now, even though I haven't said a thing. "Stop acting like a spoiled child, Park Sam Hae. And no sad face!"

She says this in Korean, even though her English is a lot better than my Korean. She says she only ever speaks Korean when we're together because that way I won't lose my heritage. She means her heritage because South Korea is where she grew up.

Not me. I've never been there. Don't even know a single Korean person, except her.

I think the real reason she does this isn't to make me get better at speaking her language. It's just so other people won't know what we're talking about.

As if anyone cares. They're just trying to get to somewhere else. As fast as possible. While more or less ignoring everyone else.

Which is what we're doing. Though I think it's fun to look at other travellers and make up stories about who they are and where they're going. And why.

And what might happen next.

It helps to pass the time.

I don't ever share these thoughts, or any thoughts,

with my mother. She'll just say it's stupid. That I don't need to think. Just do what she says and we'll both be fine. She's always telling me that.

The line shuffles forward a few feet. My mother shoves her tote bag along with one foot, not even looking up from her phone screen.

I have my violin case over one shoulder and my new backpack over the other. You can't kick them along in line.

Or you could, I guess. If you didn't care about them.

The airport we're in is the one in Paris. But it could be any airport in any city. In any country. Anywhere. They all look the same to me.

And sound the same.

And smell the same.

They all have the same shops with the same stuff that costs too much and moving sidewalks and shuttle busses or trains to get from one terminal to another.

The only real difference is what languages the signs and announcements are in. And what kind of money you have to use, if you even use actual money. Which you usually don't because debit cards and credit cards work everywhere.

Airports are nothing more than a useful tool, my mother says. It's high time I get used to travelling intelligently and using the tools responsibly. Soon, very soon, we'll be travelling constantly, to piano and violin competitions. And then, when we're successful in winning them, to guest appearances to perform.

one

With only the world's top orchestras, she adds. Because that's the life she says awaits us.

And I better start being smart about it.

It's her plan. That I'm a successful musician, a virtuoso on both piano and violin. What she calls "world-class." Performing everywhere. And she is my manager and constant companion.

I will travel and practice music, as I do now. And play. And be beautiful and gracious and smile all the time and be shiny and perfect.

And modest.

She'll do everything else. "All the real work of making a successful music career," as she puts it in Korean.

Because that's what musically-gifted prodigies are born to do. And can, if they're lucky enough to have a mother like mine to, as she says, "make the best possible success happen."

Even if, like me, they're not really sure they want this. After all, I didn't choose to be a prodigy. I don't think of myself that way. It was just kind of an accident that I'm good at music. Though I love music and can't imagine living without it, I'm not sure I want to do all this travelling and performing all the time. Spending every day, or just about every day in airports and on planes. Or trains.

Always rushing to somewhere else to get to another hall, another piano, another stage, another orchestra, another audience.

Playing is the good part. I enjoy playing music. It

makes me happy when the audience enjoys it, too.

It's all the other parts of this future I don't much like.

Always trying to get around in different cities, staying in different hotels, sleeping on different beds, talking to different people. Never quite sure of where you are right now.

Always rushing from here to there.

Never, or just about never, being at home.

Where I have my piano, my room, my things. My friends. Tia Margaret. And Tippy, my puppy. Everyone I love.

I miss them. Which isn't even worth mentioning to my mother. Because this is the life she wants for us. The life she says she's made so many sacrifices for and worked so hard for, because it's what we're meant to have. Worth what she calls, "minor inconveniences necessary to gain important achievements and reap major rewards in life."

So that's her plan for her life. And mine. Everything's already decided.

Before enjoying all the big rewards, she says, I still have so much to learn.

She doesn't mean music repertoire, which is all the pieces I know how to play and I'm learning now. She says she pays my teachers to be in charge of that.

I must work harder to be more charming with people. And not have my own opinions, because nobody wants to hear them.

one

I must be more of the dutiful daughter she expects. Stop being so willful.

Listen to her because she knows best.

Her words, not mine.

Every internationally-acclaimed artist must master the skills of calm and self-control, she says. Playing well is never enough. Virtuosos must also know how to talk to all kinds of people. How to dress. How to smile. How to have pretty hair.

And how to move efficiently and effectively through airports. And conduct myself properly at all times.

I guess she knows, because she was going to be an opera singer. Was one, for a while. Except her parents said she also had to go to university and become a lawyer. So, she gave up on her singing career. But then she never went back to work in their family's business, back in Korea. I don't know why.

I'll ask them. If I ever meet them.

Margaret says she has no idea what the answer is. She says she'd tell me if she knew.

It's the kind of question that could bring on a mother meltdown, so I don't ask. She'd only say that it is very rude to speak about yourself which, in Korean culture, is true.

Safer for me to just concentrate on what she's been teaching me to do for as long as I can remember. About music, about making famous orchestra conductors want to work with you, about airports.

About sit up straight, smile and play.

There are many necessary tools to success.

We must use the tools in the smartest ways.

We must always stride through airports quickly. With purpose. Eyes directly ahead. Face neither smiling nor unsmiling.

Never looking confused. Or lost. Or upset.

Never slowing down, except to wait in another line or at the departure gate.

Always remaining on guard.

Trusting no one.

These are the airport rules.

Another rule is, if you need something from your backpack, go into the women's room and lock the cubicle door. That's for safety if you need to get out money or a credit card or something.

Or go into one of the airport restaurants and order a drink or a snack. There, it's natural to look in your bag. No one will notice.

Never smile. Avoid looking directly at anyone. Never talk to anyone unless you have to.

At security, only answer questions you are asked. The answer must be as short as possible. Usually, a simple "yes" or "no" is best.

That, at last, is what we do. We show our boarding passes, but they only ever ask Mom questions and ignore me. After all, I'm just the kid.

Umma goes ahead of me, putting her phone and

one

laptop in one of the grey plastic containers that look like a big kitty litter pan. She plunks her plain tote bag with her new designer handbag hidden inside one and her laptop and phone in another. She arranges her suede jacket into a third one.

I do pretty much the same – violin case in one, backpack in another, laptop and phone in the third along with my sweater.

As our possessions trundle along the conveyor and into the machine to be x-rayed, my mother steps through the security arch. A woman guard waves a wand around her, nods for her to move aside and gestures to me to step forward.

I'm dreading what usually comes next, which is the red alarm going off. That always leads to questions. It's usually because of my violin. It's old. The glue that it's made with can be a problem for these security people and their technology.

But that doesn't happen this time. The bins with our stuff reappear, having passed their photography test inside the machine. We collect our belongings. Mom puts her coat on. I tuck my laptop back into my backpack.

I sigh with relief. My mother is already charging to the right and towards the departure gate for our flight to Rome. She doesn't notice that I have to race to catch up.

I don't know how she can do this, on a hot day. She's got that big tote bag and is wearing her jacket and stiletto booties. But I'm just glad I don't have to wear them.

It's a relief to finally get to our departure gate, all the way at the end of one endlessly long tentacle of this terminal. As we race-march past restaurants and magazine stands and bookstores and a kiosk selling snacks and another one with sunglasses and scarves, I wish we could stop. But my mother strides forwards. Super-charged to get there.

I have no choice but to keep up.

At last, we're sitting down, with an hour to go before our plane boards.

There are dark circles under her eyes. I don't think it's because her make-up smudged. She takes out her laptop, saying something about having some work to do, though it looks to me like she's just fiddling around online.

I could be doing the same. Instead, I offer to go get her a coffee, thinking that might make her feel better. It's a relief to get away for a few minutes. To just walk normally.

I buy a sandwich, chocolate milk and a chocolate bar for on the plane. I get a small fruit salad and a plastic fork for my mother and pull my credit card out of my jeans pocket to pay. No need to look confused or hesitant, fishing about in my bag for money.

Usually, my mother would make a fuss about me eating chocolate and what she calls junk food. "Very bad for your skin," she says. "Makes your hair dull. And you get fat. All very bad for any world-class performer."

When you're a performing artist, my mother says,

one

appearance matters. You have to look really beautiful for people to like your music.

This doesn't make a lot of sense to me, but it would be pointless to say so. She's older than me. She used to sing. She knows.

I hand her the salad and coffee, which she accepts with a nod, then sets it down and ignores it. I'm free, for a while, to just sit here and watch people.

And think back on these past few weeks.

How they zoomed by.

Learning music with Madame Boulanger and living at her big sunny Paris apartment with her daughters and what she calls her other "darling and brilliant jeunes filles." She means her students, like me.

I love it there. Loved it. Awake at dawn. Practicing, then breakfast at the little café across the street. There are always baguettes and jam and gorgeous pastries and sweet tea. We joke and laugh and talk about music.

Piano and violin lessons are in the mornings with Madame, who is brilliant. She has a way of making you play better than you ever thought you could.

"Sam, ma chère," Madame says one day, "Every artist must find her own voice. Have you found yours yet? I wonder…"

I ask her what she means but she just waves the question away with a smile. "The Chopin now, I think. Nocturne No. 6, s'il te plait." That means please.

And so, I play this lovely night music. Wondering if

Madame is hearing it with my voice, or the composer's?

Some days I practice again in the afternoons. But most days there also are outings to see and hear Paris. It's a huge, beautiful, thrilling place packed with sights. And sounds. And fun things to do. Especially when you can see it with Amélie and Katharina and Ghislaine, who are Madame's other students living with her right now, like me. And Josette and Bernadette. They're two of her daughters.

Of all of us I'm the youngest. But they never treat me that way.

We work hard. There's just something about Madame that makes you want to stretch your hands and your mind and your heart. Every time I play for her, I want it to be my personal best.

We work hard, but we're allowed to have fun, too. One afternoon, we go ice skating at the Eiffel Tower, then climb to the second level to catch the elevator all the way to the top, where from the deck you can see all of Paris spread out around us. We take lots of selfies.

We go to find the narrowest street in Paris. It's Rue du Chat qui Pêche. That means Fishing Cat Street. That name just makes me laugh, but I don't know how a little street got called this. It's barely wider than a sidewalk and far too narrow to drive a car.

Amélie, Josette and Bernadette can put their hands on a house wall at one side of Fishing Cat Street and their feet on the other, balancing themselves as they arch their bodies over the street, which is hilarious.

one

We take pictures of them doing this. I'm not tall enough to reach from one side to the other like they can, but maybe next year, peut-être?

Yes, I think. Why not? I love the way they think that we'll all be together again. Next year. I hope so.

Another day we take the train to Versailles to wander through the palace of the French kings and queens, pretending to be real princesses and oohing and ahhing about what it would be like to wear silk dresses and live in such splendour.

Other days, we go to the Louvre and join a treasure hunt. And take an opera tour for kids. Which makes us tease each other about if we'd ever write operas? And what they'd be about.

One really hot afternoon we go to Disneyland Paris.

We ride the underground. Or Josette and Amélie, who are old enough to drive, take us on their scooters. We cling to them as we speed around Paris!

Katharina is from Germany. Amélie is Polish and Ghislaine is Canadian. The one language everyone but me can speak, and Madame teaches in, is French. Being with them every day and doing everything together makes it easy for me to learn. Soon I'm chattering away and laughing with them all and loving every minute. In French.

I overhear bits of conversation on the streets and, to my surprise, I can understand what people are saying! I even dream in French.

Of course, it couldn't have happened if my mother had been there. But she'd deposited me and my suitcase at Madame's door and gone off for what she called a "romantic vacation" with her new boyfriend.

They were going to "experience Paris," my mother said. "Luis Vuitton and all the other fancy shops. Maybe get married here!"

That didn't happen. Instead, Mother came back to collect me from Madame's early. I was hoping to stay for the rest of the summer. But no, I have to hear all about what a jerk her new boyfriend is. How he just doesn't get women. And how can he be so selfish and stupid?

Plus, she thinks he took some money from her. She's gone to the police, but they just shrugged and said there is nothing to be done, madame. He used a false name, also no doubt a false passport, what chance would they have of finding him?

This is pretty much like every boyfriend she has. They never last long.

Sadly, instead of more time with the jeunes filles and music lessons with Madame and going to concerts every evening to fill ourselves up with music, as Madame says, now we have to go to Rome.

Ugh.

It's not Rome's fault.

Rome is a city in Italy. The capitol of the old Roman empire. Where the Coliseum is and they used to have gladiator fights. There's also a lot of art there. And really old buildings, older than Paris. Vesuvius is the volcano that blew up in ancient times. It buried the whole city of Pompeii in just one day. The ruins are

one

close to Rome. I'd like to see it sometime. That's about all I know about Rome.

Except that also, right now, my father's there. With his new family. He's making a movie there. That's what he does. He used to be an actor. But now he directs movies. Usually he does that kind of movie where there's lots of swearing and everyone has guns. He did one last year with Tom Cruise in it. I didn't go see it. But some kids in my class said it was pretty cool.

They didn't know it was my dad who made it. He doesn't have the same last name as me. If I said anything about him being my dad, they'd just say I was bragging. Or lying. So why bother?

I tell some people, like my real friends Morley and Jayden, that my dad lives with his new wife and new kids in California. I don't get to see him much, I say. But it doesn't really bother me. I tell them what they want to hear. Sometimes it's even almost true.

I read online that this movie my dad's making now doesn't have any car chases or fighting in it, but it does have a song in it by Lady Gaga. I wonder if I'll get to meet her. That would be so cool! But what would you say to her that everybody else doesn't say all the time, like you sing amazing and stuff like that? Or would she even be bothered to meet the director's kids?

While we wait for the plane to board, I send an email to Jayden and ask him to share it with Morley because she doesn't have a phone or a computer. And another one to Margaret. Just telling them the happy stuff.

preview

Paris was fantastic. I love lessons with Madame. It was fun, hanging out with the other girls. Now we're on our way to Rome. To see my dad. All good.

Then I send a longer, more sincere thank you to Madame, because just saying, "Hey, thanks for everything, it was great" isn't ever enough. You must send a detailed, warm-hearted written thank you when people help you. Always.

Not just because it's the thoughtful thing to do. It's because kindness matters.

I learned that from Margaret.

Continued in **Gifted**

About the Author

Jacquelyn Johnson writes books for curious and creative kids ages 8 to 12.

She used to work as a newspaper and magazine writer and editor. Her articles and photographs have appeared in newspapers and magazines in Canada, United States and Britain.

Jacquelyn is also a former teacher, college and university lecturer. She has taught English as a Second Language to children and teenagers in South Korea and journalism to university students in South Dakota and Ontario.

When not writing, she enjoys watching her garden grow while doing as little actual garden work as possible, re-decorating her home with shabby chic finds (that means fixed up used stuff, a hobby she shares with Morley's mother, Eefa) and music.

She grew up studying piano and later played the trumpet, though regrets that she has never learned to play as well as Sam Park. Or make jewellery as well as Morley. Or ride horses, like Jayden can.

She makes her home and garden with her family near the ocean in a town very much like Seabright. Just down the street from a house that's very much like Morley's. With a little cat who's very much like Feather.

Acknowledgements

I'm so grateful to Morley for coming into my life in 2019, eager to tell her story and introduce her best friends, Jayden and Sam and their world.

Thank you to CBC.ca, CBC Radio 2 and The Globe and Mail, my constant companions, for content that sparks my imagination and so often helps shape my thoughts about music, life and everything else that truly matters. I've lost count of how many times I've been thinking about a situation, or a character, or something that might happen, and exactly when I need it one of these three outstanding media present an article, opinion piece, expert interview or editorial that sparks a new story direction or gives me exactly that puzzle piece that was missing.

Thank you to Paolo Pietropaolo, writer, musician, composer, storyteller, proud immigrant and host extraordinaire of In Concert on CBC Radio 2, for talking about 'forgotten' composers, whose works deserve to be played more often, so many of whom are women. This planted the seed for a critical scene between Umma and Sam in this series and showed me another side to each of their characters.

Thank you to the composers who give or gave us their music. There are the big names every classical music lover knows, deservedly famous: Beethoven, Bach, Brahms, Chopin, Shubert, Haydn and the rest of the boys. But also those women composers so deserving

acknowledgements

of our ears, namely Clara Wieck Schumann, Louise Farrenc, Fanny Mendelssohn Hensel, Ethyl Smyth, Barbara Pentland, Alma Deutscher, Barbara Strozzi and many more. The list of accomplished musicians and composers who are women is long and varied.

As I was writing these stories, I was listening to the music mentioned and many other composers and their works, drawing inspiration, courage and strength from music of beauty and genius. We are all fortunate to live in an age when music is more celebrated, more performed and more available than to any earlier generation, for which I am profoundly grateful.

I must also mention my appreciation for online translation, shoring up my very rusty and rickety French and practically non-existent Spanish.

I truly believe that parenting is the most difficult job ever invented that is reserved exclusively for amateurs. That said, I've known parents who, for a variety of reasons, just aren't as good at the job as they need to be. Many experts have helped in my understanding of such parents and why they behave as they do. Special thanks to Dr. Lindsay C. Gibson for her books that provided profound insights into some of the characters in this series: **Understanding Emotionally Immature Parents** and **Adult Children of Emotionally Immature Parents.**

I have two long-ago teachers to thank for encouraging my writing. One is the inspiration for Mr. Cadeau in this book, though quite changed from the original. She is Sondra Bugg, my homeroom teacher in grade 8, when I was a year older than Sam, Morley and Jayden are in Sam's Christmas. I long ago lost touch with

acknowledgements

Mrs. Bugg who was my teacher at Jack London Junior High School [now Jack London Middle School] in Wheeling, Illinois, USA, but often think of her with fondness and gratitude.

As a young, confused middle-school student, it takes just one person to believe in you, the value of who you are and who you are becoming. Middle school years, as someone has said (and I wish I remembered who) is just one humiliating event after another. It is not these usually small gaffes that matter, but the building of confidence to right or overcome them. Today, we call this building skills in resilience.

Back then, no one really talked about helping kids learn how to be either confident or resilient. My Grade7/8 teacher Mrs. Bugg knew this intuitively. It was her character and kindness that have stayed with me. She likely shored up the shaky confidence of dozens of confused kids, perhaps hundreds, over the course of her teaching career. She's probably can't remember most of their names or faces. It could be that she never really realized the value of what she did. I am one who will never forget what she gave me and doubtless many others.

There are also friends to thank for the many ways they encourage and inspire. One in particular I want to thank here for being such a good friend; always interested in what I'm writing since the day we met 25 years ago. She is Dale Wilcox, a bright light in my life.

Another is my dear friend Woody Wentzy, inspiration for Gus in this series.

acknowledgements

Without the help and support of my husband and son, there would be no books completed, published and available to read. I am the most fortunate of writers to have such a loving team around me, helping to see that these stories reach you.

Like the Star family in the Morley books, my family and I run a bed and breakfast, though, sadly, it lacks a piano. Also like them, ours is a small town near the ocean popular with tourists and arty types. Seabright is not a copy of the town where I live, but a reflection of the many small, warm and welcoming towns and villages strung like a necklace of sea glass along the Atlantic coast of the United States and Canada.

These are very special places to live and work, write and play and I urge you to visit, if you ever get the chance. And if you're really lucky, perhaps you will come to stay!

CPSIA information can be obtained
at www.ICGtesting.com
Printed in the USA
LVHW050951210423
744999LV00014B/133